Sleep Is for the Rich

Sleep Is for the Rich

Donald MacKenzie

HOUGHTON MIFFLIN COMPANY BOSTON

1971

**MIDNIGHT
NOVEL OF
SUSPENSE**

For Anne Barrett and her Sophie & Paul

Sleep Is for the Rich

Chapter One

IT WAS THE END of one of those sad days between Christmas and New Year. Wet snow had been falling outside since early that morning. King's Road was a canyon filled with mud-spattering vehicles and miserable pedestrians. Sophie and I had been watching television since six o'clock. I'd cut the sound down to a whisper and turned off the living room lights. Snow whirled around the floodlit power station on the far side of the river. Now and again the thin wail of a tug's siren penetrated into the room. We were warmed by a heater disguised as an oak log, and there was an illusion of well-being. It wasn't that much of an illusion. A two-room apartment is no place for peaceful coexistence with a seven-year-old daughter. I could barely remember the alternative. Sophie's mother had been a hostess in Millie Mandler's Downtown Frolics. The marriage that had followed her positive pregnancy test was about the biggest mistake either of us could have made. We separated exactly fourteen hours afterward. I didn't see her again till she appeared in a hired car a couple of years later. "Learn all about responsibility!" she'd quipped, and dumped a small female with wet pants on me. Then she vanished into the night. Forty minutes later she was on her way to Australia with a water-pump salesman. Nobody has heard of her since.

The only relatives I had were back in Canada and their ranks had closed on me firmly twenty years before. There was no room in those Empire Loyalist strongholds for a daughter of mine. In fact, there was no room for her anywhere except with me. I had come to be glad of it. Sophie and I managed somehow, rasping one another's nerves occasionally yet establishing an oddly secure relationship. She was bright and obstinate, rarely cute, and as faithful as a Labrador.

I kept my eyes on the box, memory following the ancient cartoons, the fatuous antics of the dog detective.

"Dougal's a creep," Sophie said in a flat voice. The finality in her voice destroyed the dog forever. She was sitting with her legs tucked under her, her chin propped in her hand. "A creep," she repeated, taken with the sound of the word.

I switched the set off. "Then we don't have to watch him, do we?" It was a good lead-in to the supper-bath-bed routine. I thumbed down a button on the wall. The room was shabby in the light of the bracket lamps. Patches of damp darkened the Regency striped wallpaper. My apartment was no worse than any of the others. The whole building was due for demolition. Truth was, the place was a sorry refuge for second-rate people. Plaster was falling in the lobby downstairs. The elevators rattled up and down despairingly, as if each trip would be the last. The porters no longer pretended to take messages. Fortunately enough, the general air of apathy and indifference extended to the rental office. The clerks there accepted any kind of outrageous excuse for nonpayment of rent with sullen indifference. They too were due for the ax. I owed nine months' rent. The way things were going, it looked as if I'd still be owing it when the building was torn down. I'd lived in Thames Court for five years.

The furnished apartment consisted of a living room, a bedroom, a bath, and a kitchen. Someone must have called Feinbaum's Furniture Store a generation ago and said: "Fifty apartments, Sam, and you get the business. I want these flats to be homes, Sam, know what I mean? How much I want to spend? — Look, we've known one another long enough not to argue over money. Not a penny more than one and a half a unit. I said homes, not Buckingham Palace." The carpets and furnishings bore the scars left by countless cavalier tenants. The central-heating system clanked but it still put warmth into the building. The elevators were no more than ten yards away from my front door. The kitchen opened onto a service staircase. Throw up a window, crawl a few yards over a flat roof, and you were in the neighboring block. These things can matter. I called to my daughter from the kitchen.

"What do you want for supper, sweetheart?"

She followed her arm around the door with her nose. People say that she looks like me. There are times when I think I can see it. She's blond, her hair's straight, and her eyes are the same sort of butcher's-apron blue. The way she uses them for effect is strictly from her mother.

"A tuna-fish sandwich and a black currant yogurt," she announced.

I closed the refrigerator. She knew its contents as well as I did and never asked for anything that we didn't have. When you're as broke as I was, it's a nice touch.

"I'll join you," I said.

Sophie carried plates and the tray into the living room. I drew the curtains, blocking the view of the people who live across the well in the building. Colonel and Mrs. Scribner had been watching us closely since my arrest and trial the previous year. The fact that I had been acquitted had not satisfied their suspicions. The day after I hit the street again, the colonel made a phone call to the Welfare Department. A buck-toothed spinster showed up with a notebook and a professed concern about my daughter's adenoids and morals. It took me thirty hectic seconds to assure the lady that I was capable of supervising both. The Scribners continued their surveillance undaunted. Much of it was conducted through pearl-handled opera glasses leveled across the air shaft.

Sophie and I were working on the yogurt when the phone rang. My involuntary start almost dislocated my neck. The only people who called my number these days were irate bookmakers and debt collectors. And this was eight o'clock at night. All the old doubts and fears scrambled for recognition.

I wondered whose voice I'd hear if I lifted the phone off the hook. Would it be Inspector Uhuh from Chelsea Police Station asking me to call around and help them out in a few routine inquiries?

Sophie spoke through a mouthful of food. "The phone's still ringing, Papa."

The room was suddenly overpoweringly hot, and I dragged down the knot in my tie and unbuttoned my collar. Then I lifted the receiver and gave my number cautiously.

An assured Cockney voice came on the line. "Henderson? It's Crying Eddie, mate. Look, I'm on the blower for the big fellow. He wants to see you. Do you understand my meaning?"

The "big fellow" was Chalice, the gypsy wonder, and Crying Eddie, a tough young man with an uncompromised loyalty to his chief.

"What's he want?" I asked guardedly.

"He'll tell you himself. He wants you over here as soon as possible." Crying Eddie's tone of command made it obvious that no one had considered the possibility that I might refuse.

I looked down at the meager spread on my lap. "I'm in the middle of dinner."

"He says he's in the middle of dinner," Crying Eddie said to someone else. His voice was lost as he covered the mouthpiece and then it was clear again. "He wants to know how soon you can make it, then? Half an hour — an hour?"

I checked my watch. "Half after nine at the earliest and I don't go to nightclubs anymore." What I had in mind was the Mayfair hangout that Chalice had bought for his girl friend. The Heavy Mob used it. I couldn't have afforded to buy a round of drinks in the place, but the statement had a ring of independence.

"You don't have to go to no clubs," Eddie said shortly. "You come straight here — Chalice's gaff. I'll tell the porters downstairs."

I cradled the dead phone and poured myself a large Scotch. It was a nice exit line. Chalice lived in one of the best guarded apartment blocks in Northwest London. The owner of the liquor store in the lobby was going broke with the rest of us. I rinsed the empty glass and came back into the living room.

"I have to go out for a while, honey."

"I heard," Sophie said calmly. She was a good woman to live with. There were no recriminations. No warnings about late nights and drinking. I touched her ear fondly. "You want me to get Joan to come up and sit for a while or will you be O.K. alone?"

A couple of Australian girls ran a baby-sitting service from their apartment downstairs. Sophie liked them.

"I'll be O.K.," she said casually. "I'll stay here and read." Reading consists of tearing a newspaper in strips, chatting away to herself as she does so. If you listen closely, the story line is clear. There's this little girl who lives in a clearing in a forest with two ponies and a goat that talks. Sophie usually falls asleep before she reaches the climax. I hurried her into the bath. The routine had long since become familiar. Test the water with the elbow, lay the pajamas on the radiator, stripe the toothbrush with paste. I dried her and carried her into the bedroom. Her cot stands by my bed. I gave her the racing sheet to read. The kind of job I was doing picking winners it seemed a good choice for destruction.

She lifted her face to be kissed. The moment never failed to turn me into a defiant dreamer. No one was going to take her away from me. The old fantasy flared in my brain. One day there'd be a home somewhere in the country and a governess for Sophie. The years jumped and a tall Icelandic beauty was pouring tea on the lawn for her adored father.

"Stay away from the power switches," I warned. "And if the phone rings, don't answer it. Promise?"

She was already engrossed in her tearing and nodded abstractedly. We don't lie much to one another and most of the time we fulfill our contracts.

I cut all the lights except one in the bedroom. The Aussie girls were at home downstairs, drinking beer from the bottle. I left them the key to my apartment. Joan promised to look in on Sophie later. Strips of burlap were laid in the lobby, protecting the dingy carpet from the filth being tracked in from outside. Wet snow was still falling in the street. I waited for a cab. George, the night porter, has a number that works in any kind of weather.

I hadn't bothered to change. I was presentable in cavalry-twill pants, a suede jacket, and a beaver-lined overcoat from Toronto days. As Pretty Sid used to say, there's only a few of us left. I did a double take on that one, wondering what made me think of him. Sid was sitting somewhere in a French jail and would be for the next ten years.

George signaled from the doorway. I ducked into the cab and leaned back, closing my eyes. There is a natural order in the world of thieves. Topflight burglars nod to good con men; the bank and bullion robbers acknowledge the share-pushers. At that level there's a kind of freemasonry. The only qualifications necessary are success and a reputation for solidity. There had been a time when I had both. Harry Chalice's life was legendary. He'd been born in a caravan and raised by a horse-stealing father. He'd taught himself to read and write while ducking the truancy officers. At sixteen he'd lied himself into the Seventh Army, picked up three medals for bravery in action over the next four years, and finished his war in detention barracks. It was the last time that the key would be turned on him. For the next twelve years or so he master-minded assaults on bullion shipments, three airport robberies, and countless payroll heists. An elder statesman of crime, he had a 500-acre farm in Ireland, a paper mill in Essex, and a numbered bank account in Zürich. Drunks on temporary leave-of-absence from the big house sobered up at the mention of his name, and the cops referred to him with a kind of frustrated respect. I'd been involved in a deal with him three years before. Some of his team had stumbled on a box full of Canadian bearer bonds that I'd been able to unload at a thrifty 17 per cent discount.

I knew Chalice to be a shrewd, loyal, and determined leader who controlled a handful of picked associates. His clothes were made on Savile Row, his shirts tailored by Sulka. Any time he thought he might display ignorance, he kept his mouth shut. He read Bond and Boswell, improving his grasp on realities if not his grammar. He had made Crying Eddie, and Eddie never forgot it.

The coming interview gave me a mixed feeling of excitement and apprehension. I hadn't turned a trick in sixteen months and we were slowly starving. My one brush with the law had left me badly shaken. I'd been hit with a number of propositions since then. Most of them were of the kind where the guy eases up and offers some vague bit of information he's either read or heard. More rarely the tips were professional, offering an evaluation of the loot, its position, and the protective measures taken. I'd been turning them all down without exception, inventing reasons that I knew didn't exist. Finally nobody came around anymore; nobody called. I told myself I was glad. The real truth was that I wasn't sure how much nerve I had left.

Chalice's summons seemed to crystallize my position, the hopelessness of trying to go on as I was, my lack of confidence. I had a hunch that I was on the threshold of something really big. The one thing I was certain of was that with

8

Chalice any larcenous caper would be as safe as it could be.

I opened my eyes on the cab's steamed-up windows. Beyond the swishing arcs of the windshield wipers I could see the lights of the Outer Circle. The hack slackened its speed almost immediately and pulled up in front of a canopied entrance. The apartment building where Chalice lived faced Regent's Park.

A doorman wearing a gleaming slicker held an umbrella over me as I paid off the driver. A quarter-inch thickness of plate glass insulated the hushed lobby against the feathers of melting snow. The second hand of a clock behind the reception desk swept around silently. The porters beneath it were gray-grave and watchful.

"Mr. Chalice's apartment," I said. "I'm expected."

The man's eyes snapshotted me for the record. He opened the doors on a bronze-faced elevator cage. "The top button, sir. It's express to the penthouse."

A giant hand plucked the cage upward. I used the mirror to give a little shape to my salt-and-pepper hair. The Spanish tan had faded to a dirty putty color and I'd put on weight over the last few months. I looked away before the here-I-am-all-washed-up-at-thirty-eight routine took over again.

The elevator cage stopped with the precision of an expensive watch. There was no jar, no clatter; nothing more than a faint click and then the doors rolled back silently. The front door immediately behind the gate looked impregnable to anything short of a bulldozer. There was a circle of optic glass set in the door at shoulder level. A blue eye showed there, cold and disembodied. Then the door opened and shut behind me. Crying Eddie took my topcoat. He was built on the order of a good welterweight in training, with small flat ears pressed tightly against his skull. His brown hair was neatly dressed in a side parting. He was wearing a fringed antelope jacket over a flame-colored silk shirt, and brown-and-black checked trousers. He led the way down a thick-carpeted corridor hung with old prints of prize fighters, put my coat in a closet, and turned gracefully.

"You're sure nobody was on your tail, mate?"

He's got a lot of style for his age. It rubs people the wrong way occasionally.

"I'm not a boy burglar," I said casually.

His eyes narrowed but he jerked his head and I followed. Crying Eddie worries about a number of things. If he can't find a subject that will occupy his mind, he worries about that, too. He's concerned with his blood pressure, the probity of banks, and his aged mother's raids on his small change.

He ushered me into a room the size of a tennis court. It was divided into two levels by three steps. The upper half was a sort of library with a profusion of books. Electrically controlled windows offered a panoramic view of the Hampstead heights. There was no need to draw the curtains. There was no one to look in. The distant lights were blurred and snow pattered against the windowpanes softly.

Chalice heaved himself up from a suede-upholstered sofa. He had grown sidewhiskers since the last time I'd seen him. It seemed to me to be the definitive touch, adding the final note of piracy to his swarthy face. He was elegantly draped in brown hopsacking and wore wing-tip shoes bearing the boned luster of the handmade article. The bristle of hair over peaked eyebrows had grown somewhat grayer. He put his hand out in greeting.

"Hi, Paul, mate. How've you bin?"

His interest sounded genuine. I turned my palm over a

couple of times. "Up and down. I've been taking things fairly easy."

A contour map was hanging on the wall behind him, showing a lake and houses. The legend underneath read TODTSEE.

Chalice nodded as he noticed my interest. "Later, mate!" He kicked a log in the fireplace and leaned his shoulder blades against the mantel. He scratched away luxuriously, watching me.

I guess I'd always taken it for granted that if people lived in a penthouse and wanted to burn oak logs it would be arranged. But at that moment there was something a little unreal about it all. It wasn't only the neatly stacked logs fifteen stories up in the air — it was the suede-upholstered furniture, the lacquered cabinet that had been turned into a drinks cupboard, the shelves filled with beautifully made toy soldiers. Crying Eddie started moving ice in a shaker. Chalice smiled.

"I knew you'd been resting, mate. I mean I heard about your bit of bovver."

It seemed an odd way of referring to a prosecution that could well have put me behind bars for years. Guilty I'd certainly been, but I'd sworn that if the Fate Sisters just listened to me once, I'd take the pledge. As it was, a hung jury had saved my neck.

"Oh, that," I said largely. "You know the way it goes, Harry."

His eyebrows joined, a solid bar of bristles. "Scotch all right?"

I took the glass that Crying offered. The Waterford tumbler was a far cry from my own Woolworth ware. Chalice was drinking Scotch, Crying his usual milk.

"Cheers," said Chalice, and wiped his mouth. We all drank solemnly. The protocol on such occasions is formal. Crying Eddie was sitting on the sofa watching Chalice like a terrier that knows that it's going to be asked to perform tricks.

"Phil Cody, of all people. How'd you come to get lumbered with a slag like that, Paul, boy?"

The name was an insult in Chalice's mouth. The truth was that I *had* been lumbered. Cody's treachery had taken the form of a lively piece of queen's evidence. Nevertheless I wasn't too happy about being reminded of it. I shrugged.

"I was conned. There's always a first time."

It took a few seconds for Chalice to hand down his verdict. "There didn't ought to be, mate. Not in our business. *I* ain't never been conned, for example."

Crying Eddie's voice was insultingly bland. "What's that bird of yours been doing for the last three years, then?"

If my head was going to be open and inspected, I thought, then a little sarcasm would not be out of place.

"You're an exceptional fellow, Harry."

He moved away from the fire and perched on the end of the sofa. His dark eyes brooded over what I'd said.

"You don't change, do you, mate," he said finally. "You ain't got a pot to piss in, but you still act the lord of the bleedin' manor."

I felt the blood rising over my collar. "Let's start by talking about the last time I asked you for anything, Harry."

He accepted the rebuff without rancor. "Fair enough, mate. No, you ain't never asked me for nothing. Nor anybody else as far as I know. You're a getter, not an asker. Have another drink."

I held my glass out. The Scotch took the edge from my resentment. I told myself to cool it. Crying Eddie tilted the bottle, pouring as if he was surrendering his life's blood.

Chalice knuckled through the stubble of graying hair, his voice testy.

"For crissakes, give him the bottle and sit down, Ed. Now listen to me, Paul. You're about the best I know at your lark and yet you let a slag like that Cody near ruin you. Don't you know that when the pressure's on bastards like him run true to form? Of *course* he was going to open his mouth as soon as his collar was felt! Of course he'd give queen's evidence. I could have told you all that."

The airy certainty in his voice needled me. "It didn't occur to me at the time to ask your advice," I said stubbornly. "It was Cody's job. All the signs were right."

Eddie's head sank a little lower on his neck at what was doubtless treason in the throne room. But Chalice was unperturbed. He answered mildly.

"I was only making a point, mate. The point being you nearly went inside. Now take me, for instance. I ain't done a day's bird since the army. You know why? That's when I got religion, mate. There I was running around in this compound in Naples in battle dress, ninety in the shade, carrying fifty pounds of old iron on me bleedin' back! There was this staff sergeant who'd sit under a sunshade with a bucketful of piss. As fast as one of us would fall down, he'd empty the bucket over our heads. He was a true gentleman, Staff Sergeant Phillips, and he taught me a lot. He taught me the importance of trusting someone, Paul. There was two hundred of us in that compound and only twenty-five of them. It wasn't the guns and the wire that made the difference.

They trusted one another and we didn't. How much do you think I'm worth?"

The question took me completely by surprise. "You mean money?"

"Altogether," he smiled.

I tried adding what I knew and got nowhere. I hedged. "You're not short of a dollar."

The answer seemed to please him for some reason. "That's right, mate. In fact me and Ed don't need to do a stroke for the rest of our naturals. We got an accountant with five letters after his name who says so. But there's more than just money in life, there's the glory and the respect. That's what I want, mate. People to remember me with respect. There ain't much of it left in this country. England's going to the bleedin' dogs, Paul. All these young tearaways putting people into bacon-slicing machines, electric wires up their arses, and all that. They're no better than cannibals, that's what. The law's against them, the public's against them, and they're against one another. No wonder the judges are handing out life sentences. And so they should. Me, I'd string the bastards up."

He crossed to the fireplace again, spat into the flames, and wiped his lips on a silk handkerchief.

"Excuse me," he said punctiliously, and flung his arm out in a dramatic gesture. "I love my country, mate. It's the only one I know but I love it. I always wanted my last big score to be right here in England. But all them thugs have made it impossible. England ain't safe anymore, so I've shifted the scene of battle, Paul. And there it is!"

He jerked his head back at the relief map on the wall. Crying Eddie was silent, staring into his glass of milk.

"Battle," I repeated.

I guess I must have smiled, for his tone sharpened. "What's so bleedin' funny about it?" he demanded. I shook my head, but he wagged a monitory finger at me. "Don't tell me you're like Eddie, laughing out of ignorance. You've had education and you ought to know better. *Battle*'s what I said. You're going into battle every time you climb through some old bird's bedroom window, and don't never forget it. And when you go into battle you've got to have organization and leadership. That's if you're not operating alone. More than that, you've got to have confidence in your partners. Right?"

"Right," I agreed. He seemed to be on the verge of making his pitch.

Crying Eddie's face was closed tight, his eyes unwinking.

"Well then," said Chalice, "I'm going to tell you what I'm offering, mate. I'm offering you the chance to come in on the biggest score of the century. Correct, Ed?"

His partner nodded. "The biggest score." His voice held a certain reluctance, or it seemed so to me.

Chalice continued. "One of these days people are going to wake up and look at their newspapers. Know what they're going to see there? The biggest jewel robbery of all time, that's what! And it'll be done by the three of us, mate. Me, you, and him. And the important thing is that nobody's ever going to be able to prove it."

I put my empty glass down and leaned back. "What are we taking — the Crown jewels?"

"Better," he said with composure. "We supply the bankroll and muscle. You supply the brains. Get the gear down, Ed. All of it."

Crying Eddie opened up a chest. He came back with his arms full and dumped the load on the sofa. There was a large carton, what looked like a tiny tape recorder, and a pile of glossy magazines — *Oggi, Jours de France, Olá, Country Life*. Chalice selected one in French. The cover displayed a dazzling blonde on an ice rink. A banner strung over her head identified the place, date, and occasion:

STOCKHOLM, 5 JANUARY 1947

WORLD ICE SKATING CHAMPIONSHIPS

He handed the magazine to me. "You speak the language. Read out loud what it says, in English."

He opened the magazine somewhere in the middle. The same face as on the cover smiled out at the photographer, twenty-three years older and wrapped in a sable hood. A legend underneath proclaimed: *Le tout-set se rassemble pour la fête de Marika!* There was a four-page spread with still more photographs. I started to paraphrase the slyly sarcastic text.

" 'The glamorous Marika Bergen, forty-eight, three times Olympic figure-skating champion, three times married to a millionaire, owner of the Munich Ice Follies . . .' There's a lot more here about her love life. You want me to go on?"

Chalice cocked his swarthy head. "How many languages can you speak, Paul?"

"Three. English, French, and German."

"You see!" he said to Crying Ed, and returned his attention to me. "You don't have to do all the words, mate. Just the bits about Bergen and Todtsee. I've heard it all before anyway. We got some old lady in Kensington to do the translations." He cocked his head again like a man listening to the sound of far-off music.

I cleared my throat. "It says she's giving an exhibition of figure skating and a gala ball afterward. She's supposed to be spending a bomb. She's rented a maharajah's mansion and everyone's going to be there: B.B.'s exes, all the unemployed royals from Estoril, a couple of Greek ship owners. She's hired bodyguards, booked whole floors in hotels for her guests, and just about taken over the town in general."

I looked up to find them both watching me intently. Chalice chose a smallish journal that was at the bottom of the pile. He read the title first, stumbling a bit:

"THE ACTUARY'S ADVISOR

ZURICH, 20 DECEMBER
Insurance circles here buzzed with the news that Marika Bergen's collection of jewelry will leave bank custody for the first time in six years. Independent valuers assessed the worth of the collection at over a million dollars in 1958. Miss Bergen's jewels include the famous *Lachryma Christae* diamond necklace, formerly the property of the Czar of Russia. The 1958 value set on the collection will have risen considerably since then. A premium of 12% is said to have been asked and paid to cover a seven-day period of complementary insurance. Special security arrangements have been made with the Slade Agency of New York."

He chucked the magazine back on the sofa. Crying Eddie stacked it neatly with the others.

"*Now* do you follow?" asked Chalice, fingering a side-whisker.

I was chasing half a dozen ideas at the same time. Each of them was fairly disturbing.

"I guess not," I answered. "That is, not entirely."

The reply brought a frown to his face. "I wouldn't have

thought it was that difficult, mate. You, me, and Eddie's going to take Bergen's loot, but that's only a starter. We're going to clear the lot — all them old birds dancing around that ballroom — Grace's gear, the royals with their tararas, and we get it all, Paul. Every bleedin' bit of it. It'll be our last coup and there's nothing to stop us. Don't tell me you're *still* not with me!"

I was, by God, and it terrified me. "Look," I said hurriedly. "Does either of you know anything at all about Switzerland? I don't mean that they make watches and shoot apples off each other's heads. I'm talking about their general social attitude."

Chalice assumed the air of a commanding officer about to be briefed by an aide.

"Tell him, Ed!"

Crying Eddie's chin cocked defiantly. I had a feeling that his regard for me was less than Chalice's.

"I know what the book said, that's all. It's this small country up in the Alps and nobody ever conquered them. There's cantons and all that, and they speak three languages — or is it four? Anyway, the rich keep their money there and lunatics go there to break their legs."

"Very good," I said. "You ought to peddle that line to the Swiss Tourist Board. I'm sure they'd appreciate it. You've missed the point, both of you. The way I understand things, you're planning the grandest sort of larceny in Switzerland. Have you any idea how the law works over there — what the cops are like?"

Chalice's hands were joined. He twiddled his thumbs comfortably. "We know enough, mate. I talked with that Joe Goss — the one who got lumbered in Berne over them traveler's checks. He said they kept him screwed up for thirteen months before they brought him to trial — wouldn't let him have no visitors, not even his old woman. Nobody but his mouthpiece. Don't worry about me, Paul. I don't underestimate no law no matter where it is. I always give Old Bill the benefit of the doubt."

I understood that this statement covered the Swiss police, cantonal and federal. I opened *Jours de France* at a spread on Bergen. One of the photographs had been shot at Kennedy Airport. It was a week or so old and showed Marika posing for the photographers. Another blonde was with her, taller and twenty years younger. Behind the two women was a trio of hard-nosed characters staring into the lens suspiciously. I held the picture up so that Chalice could see it.

"The law," I said. "Private detectives. I'd like to ask you another question — why do you think her jewelry generally stays in the bank? Don't bother answering: I'll tell *you* why. Marika Bergen's been on the list of every good burglar for fifteen years or more. The guys have taken more shots at her than you've seen football matches. She knows all the tricks, Harry, every last one of them. Any time she's not wearing it, you'll find her jewelry in a safe with six men sitting around watching it. Open the safe and there'll be another six sitting inside."

Eddie scowled into his empty glass. "Why waste your time, Harry? He's lost his nerve. I told you he had!"

"Belt up," said Chalice. "Get yourself another glass of milk or something. I've got a plan that will work, Paul. You could put a hundred cops in that mansion and it would still work. What I need from you is two things. The first is a buyer for the gear. Someone who'll guard our liberty like his own —

somebody who could find maybe half a million in cash."

He bit the end from a cheroot and lit it. His manner and voice were completely relaxed. His assurance made the statement somehow less preposterous. Van der Pouk's face clicked into my consciousness.

"There's only one guy in the world who answers that description," I told him.

Cigar smoke drifted between us. He leaned forward, brushing it away.

"I'll have to know who, Paul. Maybe not now but sooner or later."

I understood perfectly. A man like Chalice would have to know, but what could I tell him? That the only thing Van der Pouk did without artistry was paint — that two years' study in Paris had depressed him to the point of reorganizing his life completely? He had stolen a Vermeer that a South African had entrusted to him for copying. The South African had been bent on a swindle of his own. Van der Pouk had smuggled it into the States and sold it for $32,000. That was in 1939. He'd fought his war in the Belgian Congo, doubling his capital somehow in drenched mountain forests inhabited by gorillas. The war over, he appeared in Antwerp and founded Chase Fine Jewels, with branches in New York and Rio de Janeiro. Other interests were added as the years went by — timber yards, a vinegar distillery, the biggest mobile cranes on the wharves. He was vaguely married and one of the richest men in Belgium. A certain defiance of convention remained in spite of all this. Any audacious expression of it in others turned him on. For some obscure reason burglary delighted him. There was a mystique about the way one came to know him: confrontations with phony cops, checks and cross-checks till his devious brain was satisfied that one was on the level. But once you *were* in, it was like being in a burglar's paradise. Van der Pouk paid market prices for stolen property. In return he demanded a step-by-step account of the burglary. He wanted to know how the room looked, smelled, and *felt;* if the woman asleep in her bed had moved as you took the safe keys from her handbag. He once asked me whether I felt like God as I prowled through the quiet shadows. These answers seemed to satisfy some strange quirk in his make-up.

Any really fine piece of jewelry has its own passport. It is photographed by infrared rays; its color, weight, and structure are noted. Someone had once called Paulus Van der Pouk a "renaissance man manqué," a description that wasn't far off beam. Certainly he was a skilled jeweler and goldsmith. He employed a staff of thirty at Chase Fine Jewels — cutters, setters, and polishers working with the most up-to-date machinery. Van der Pouk bought hot jewelry maybe two times in a year and from five people at most. When his staff had finished for the day, he'd take his stolen property into the atelier and he'd snip, shave, and redesign till the pieces were beyond recognition. As often as not, the end product was even more beautiful than the original.

I reduced all this to the essentials and gave them to Chalice. "I'd trust him with my life, let alone my liberty," I added.

Crying Eddie smiled acidly. "It ain't your life and liberty we're worried about, mate."

Chalice's frown silenced him.

"We got a geezer on the payroll at the Yard — someone who works in the Criminal Records Office. Any time they pull the file on someone I'm interested in, I get the word. And the word is that your file's marked Inactive, mate. They got the idea you've retired, which is a right giggle under the circumstances."

I could think of nothing to say. He brought his face close to mine.

"Don't *you* think it's a right giggle, mate?"

I blinked. "Hilarious. There's something I don't quite get, Harry. It's this bit about you wanting me to supply brains. It's the first time I can remember you being so modest."

His grin took fifteen years off his age. "Well, you know what I mean. A little bit of class and polish. You've mixed with these society people. You know how to talk to them, how to behave yourself. That's what I need. Open up that box, Ed."

I stood by the sofa as Crying Eddie undid the cardboard carton. The first things out were some gas masks with extended headpieces that dropped around the shoulders. With them came elbow-length gloves of heavy-gauge rubber. Eddie extracted three cylinders from their charcoal wrappings. Each was the size of a can of tennis balls. Chalice threw one at me. I caught it hurriedly, feeling liquid slosh around inside the can.

"Nerve gas," said Chalice. "There's enough in these three cans to knock out two hundred people and not do no permanent damage. Don't ask me where it came from. It don't smell and there's no taste to it. Now give a look at what's on the wall."

The main plan was an architect's elevation of an enormous mansion. A legend dated April 1929 identified the plan as SHAHPUR, the property of His Highness the Maharajah of Srinagar.

Chalice flourished his blunt hairy fingers before letting them come to rest on the glossy paper.

"This come out of an old copy of *Country Life*. How many of them books did you look through before you found it, Ed?"

Crying Eddie's manner was resigned. "Seventy-three. Me eyesight's probably gone." Nothing would have been more unlikely. His eyes looked as if they'd spot a flea on a falcon.

Chalice moved in a wreath of cheroot smoke, pointing out one feature after another on the plan and explaining. The house had been built in the golden days of the Raj. There were twenty-five bedrooms with as many baths, quarters for a company of servants. The ballroom was a replica of the state ballroom in Srinagar Palace. There was a squash court, stabling, and a polo field. The maharajah had been accustomed to spend exactly two months in Todtsee, one in the winter, the other in the summer. A special train would haul his personnel and his animals. The house had stood empty since the end of the war, the ownership disputed by the maharajah's family and the Indian government. Marika Bergen had rented it from the latter.

Chalice lowered the aerial map. Todtsee was ringed by the great mountains of the Upper Engadine. Beyond this formidable wall, thousands of peaks pointed the way to the Austrian Alps and the Bavarian heights. I moved away from the board to the window and stood there watching the swirling feathers of snow melt as they touched the heated glass. I was thinking of Sophie, of lawns and paddocks in front of a Georgian façade. It was like some ring-rusty prize fighter facing the prospect of a comeback for the biggest prize ever.

Chalice's question jolted into my reverie. "What is it, mate? What's your problem?"

I turned around slowly. Everything in the apartment was testimony to his luck and judgment. If a guy stuck with them there could *be* no problems.

"I'm thinking about two hundred people — a house lousy with cops. And you're proposing to walk around the place spraying nerve gas like you were bombing mosquitoes. We'd be dead before we'd covered a yard, Harry."

"You should live so long," Chalice said enigmatically. "You're a scholar. Read this."

The piece of paper he gave me had been torn from a quarterly called *Frontiers of Science*. It was no more than a few lines.

New German Neurogas

Code name: LPH		
Common name: Pacifier	O	CH₃
	î	I
Chemical formula: UH₃	P	OCH
Form: odorless liquid	I	I
Form of dissemination: liquid vapor	F	CH₃

Remarks:

This gas has been widely tested. A dose of mgs. min/m₃ is sufficient, if inhaled, to render subject immobile for a minimum period of two hours. If the gas is absorbed through the skin, a considerably longer period is necessary to achieve the same effect, something in the region of five hours.

Doses in excess of twenty times that previously given will result in death.

Side effects are disruption of vision, pain in eyeballs, difficulty in respiration, constriction of pupils, etc.

I gave the piece of paper back to Chalice. He threw it in the fire.

"You plan to use this stuff, relying on that article?" I said.

"Not exactly, no, mate. As a matter of fact, we've tried it ourselves. At least Eddie has. He was out for three hours. How'd it feel, Ed?"

His partner's glance was baleful. "Why don't you try it on him — then he'd know at first hand."

Chalice waved the answer away. "No danger, Paul. What's in them cans is exactly right for the size of the ballroom and don't bother asking me how I know *that!* Minimum dose there's no danger of any permanent damage. Like they say in that piece, your eyeballs may ache and you're a bit chesty. That's all. The main thing is that sixty seconds after you take the first whiff you're on your way to dreamland. And you stay there for at least two hours."

I didn't bother challenging his expertise. There are very few authorities to which Chalice can't obtain access. I could only see one area of weakness in his plan. It was going to be almost impossible to plot movements in a house full of guests and servants. I put it to him.

"How about the guy who happens to be down in the cellar when the gas is released, or the woman in the can? All it needs is just one joker . . ." I drew my finger across my throat.

Chalice shook his head. "Don't get your bowels in an uproar, mate. There ain't going to *be* nobody walking around loose. You'll see, when the time comes."

The realization that I was running out of objections gave me a strange feeling of exhilaration. I put the last question to him.

"Todtsee is four thousand eight hundred feet above sea level and there's only one highway out of the place. It'd take over four hours by road to get to Zürich. Have you thought about that?" I knew that he had. I just wanted to hear him say it.

Crying Eddie made no secret of being bored with me. He moved his hand fastidiously.

"We flap our bleedin' wings, mate, and fly away over the mountains — that's what!"

Chalice silenced him. "There's an airport in Todtsee that's open all year round. I want you to charter a plane. We'll keep it sitting there like a taxi."

"You mean we're going to fly there?" I said doubtfully.

Chalice turned the corners of his mouth down. "No, I don't. We drive. The law'll be at that airport picking up the villains one by one as they step off the planes. I ain't as bleedin' stupid as that, mate. They're only concerned about who comes in. Their real headache will be who goes out. Follow me?"

"I follow."

"Now," said Chalice largely. "You don't have to worry about expense money. Me and Eddie's putting in ten grand apiece and there's more if it's needed. The main thing is whatever we use has got to be the best. Expenses will come off the top and we split them three ways at the sell-up. Are you in or not, mate?"

I'd known what I'd say right from the beginning. "Sure, I'm in. With one small proviso. I don't know if you realize this, but I've got a seven-year-old daughter. There's nobody who could take care of her. She'll have to come along, too. Don't worry about her, though. She minds her own business. Besides, it's like a guy who smokes a pipe — nobody with a child can be a rogue."

Eddie's handsome face registered genuine shock. "Take a little kiddy out on villainy! You must be out of your bleedin' mind, mate!"

I sank the last of the Scotch in the glass. "Let me be the judge of that! Look, Harry, I'm serious about this. Sophie and I are never parted."

Chalice's eyes were thoughtful. "I was thinking about Doll and the club, but that wouldn't do. How about your old mum, Eddie? Wouldn't she take care of the baby for a few days?"

Crying Eddie shook his head. "She wouldn't miss her bingo and the pub, mate. She never did for me, so why would she do it for someone else?"

"Look," I said stubbornly. "The whole thing's simple enough. If I go, Sophie goes." The Scotch was in my brain and what I said seemed the essence of reason.

Chalice lifted his shoulders. His surrender was completely unexpected.

"It don't make no difference to me one way or another. Bring her then. Come to think of it, perhaps you're right. A seven-year-old will make us look respectable.

"Now here's the plan, Paul. We all arrive in Todtsee by car. Eddie's the chauffeur; I'm the valet; you're this rich Canadian millionaire. We got our gear from Moss Brothers this morning. Ed looks the business: a gray tunic and breeches, a cap and an overcoat down to his ankles. I look like a coffin salesman."

At this point the phone rang. We were silent as Eddie answered it. His replies were curt and to the point. He hung up and spoke to Chalice.

"It's the garage. They want to know about the registration by nine o'clock tomorrow. I mean what name they're to give to the licensing people."

Firelight ruddied Chalice's dark face, giving it an expression of sly satisfaction.

"Do you mind having a Silver Cloud registered in your name, Paul?"

"A *Rolls?*" I said incredulously.

He moved his head. "I told you, mate — no expenses spared. We want the best of everything. I want you to remember that."

I lit a fresh butt. "You guys have left things kind of late, haven't you? This ball's only six days away and it takes us two days to reach Todtsee. That's another thing, Harry. Have you ever been in a really cold winter? Do you know what it does to your driving, for instance?"

Neither of them seemed to think the question worth answering. I put my hands on my knees and leaned forward.

"You'd better start thinking about all that. You can begin by ringing your garage first thing in the morning and having a set of snow tires fitted. And remember this, cold will affect your breathing and anything else you do."

Crying Eddie pointed his toe and sighted down his leg at it. "Can't he go home now, Harry? Tell him what he's got to do and let's wrap it up for the night. I want to get back and have a chat with my old lady."

It was the first declaration of hostilities between us. Looking at his face, at the careless challenge in it, I felt that there would be many more before we finished. Obviously there was something about me that riled him.

I stubbed out the butt in an ashtray. "It suits me if we wrap it up. I've left my kid with baby sitters."

Chalice came to his feet. "I told Monkey Farrell to ready some passports for us. You can pick 'em up in the morning."

I shook my head firmly. "You two can do what you like, but I don't travel on a crooked passport. I'll need some money, by the way."

Chalice produced fifty ten-pound notes from a gold-edged wallet. He gave the money to me.

"Just keep a note of what you spend. We'll do the figures after we score. When you've collected the passports from Monkey, see about a charter plane. Tell them we'll want it for a week and it's got to be in Todtsee the day after tomorrow."

I put the money away in an inside pocket. The phone call to me had been nothing more than a formality. My acceptance had been assumed.

"You guys seem to have been very sure of yourselves," I suggested.

Chalice wriggled one shoulder. "Yeh, well, you know! You're an artist, not a mechanic. I knew you wouldn't be able to let a job like this slip by."

Crying Eddie leaked a sarcastic smile. "Especially with all expenses paid."

I looked at him steadily. "Are you and I going to be playing this game all the time or is there a season for it?"

"I'd say all the time," he said, holding his smile.

"Cut it out," said Chalice. He gestured at the things on the sofa. "Take all that gear with you, Paul. Everything except the gas. We'll bring that. When you've got everything in your head that you want, get rid of those magazines and maps."

His manner had a strange sort of glee. He talked as if we were about to embark on a two-week hunting spree with a bunch of boozing buddies. Robbing Bergen suddenly seemed a viable project to me. I found myself considering its aspects calmly and clearly. First was the fact that I was teamed up with guys who didn't know the meaning of failure. Second was the thought that we really were going for broke — for the biggest jewel robbery of all time. The plan had a couple of obvious weak points but these were trivial enough. I shouldn't have been taking Sophie along, for instance, but where else could she go? After her mother had taken off I'd always sworn that I'd never put a frontier between Sophie and me. The other thing that faintly disturbed me was Chalice's insistence on phony passports for himself and Eddie. This kind of thing is all right if you happen to be hot. You can literally vanish in a city with the law about to pounce. But part of Chalice's spiel was that we were never going to *be* hot, in which case phony p.p.'s were nothing but an additional hazard.

Chalice screwed up his nose, blocking a yawn. "That's it, then, I'm going to bed. Don't forget to call the garage about them snow tires, Ed. Did they say how long it'd take to get the registration and insurance in the morning?"

Crying Eddie looked up from buffing his nails on the suede upholstery.

"It'll all be finished by one o'clock. Everything. I'll buy the ferry tickets in his name." He nodded in my direction.

I stuffed the magazines and maps in a canvas holdall that Chalice gave me.

"What about our cover story? What are we doing in Switzerland?"

"You tell us," suggested Chalice.

I thought for a moment. "It's best to stick as close to the truth as possible. You two are British, I'm Canadian. You got your jobs from the same agency here in London. We'll pick some name from the phone book just in case. It won't be long before people start asking you about me. Where I come from, what I do — that sort of thing. If you've just been hired, you wouldn't be expected to know too much. Be vague. I don't want to put myself in a position where some smart bastard looks me up in a reference book. All you can say is that you've been hired for a year, that my base is in Winnipeg, and you think that I have mining interests back in Canada."

Crying Eddie looked up. "And what are you going to Todtsee *for?*"

"To watch the curling. It just so happens there's an international tournament."

He turned his hand sideways, admiring the polish on his nails. "What the bleedin' hell's curling?"

"Bowls on ice," I said curtly. "If it's all right with you, Harry, I'll split."

Chalice yawned again, displaying a bank of gold crowns at the back of his mouth.

"Good night, son. Eddie'll take care of the tickets. He'll give you a ring in the morning and tell you where the meet is. Be lucky!"

He shut the bedroom door behind him firmly. I shrugged into my coat and Crying Eddie came as far as the elevator with me. He leaned against the ironwork, thumbed the button, and faced me.

"What was that you said about that tournament — something on ice?"

"Bowls," I said steadily, and spelled the word out for him.

His chin came up a fraction. "I got a strange feeling about you, Henderson. I hope it ain't right. For your sake, I hope so."

I pushed by, leaving my last word as the cage descended. "You don't turn me on either, friend, but maybe you'll grow on me."

I found a cab with one of those talkative drivers. This one was carrying on about his forthcoming holiday — two weeks in Tenerife — all that cheap booze and all them Swedish birds. I didn't even bother closing the partition. I just switched off my mind. The two Australian girls were still sitting up watching television. They reported no drama. I collected my key and rode upstairs. I made no noise going into the apartment. I've had plenty of practice. Sophie was asleep with her chum on the covers beside her. I closed the door gently and tipped the contents of the holdall onto the living room floor. For the next hour I read through every magazine article that would help me. Chalice would be asleep by now, happy that the tricky aspects of his scheme were in the hands of an expert. My feeling was that nothing was going to prove quite as easy as Chalice expected.

Bergen's house would be alive with guests, cops, and servants. And in order to plant the gas I had to get inside the place. I went over the architect's drawings again. Someone had sketched in the position of the power and telephone lines. After ten minutes' study I could have reproduced the drawings from memory. Last of all was the big spread on Bergen in *Jours de France*. A dozen or so shots had her standing beside the same woman, a tall blonde with elegant bones and a haughty manner. The text identified her as Baroness von Regensdorf, Marika Bergen's social secretary. I stored her likeness in my brain along with the rest of the information. Then I took the papers outside and burned them on the fire escape.

Sophie was sitting up in her cot when I went into the bedroom. I'm no Benjamin Spock but I've learned enough about my daughter to know that conning her is apt to backfire. I sat down on my bed.

"I've got a surprise for you."

"What is it?" she asked suspiciously.

I took my time, emptying my pockets onto the dresser. One way and another, Sophie knew enough about money. I could see her through the mirror, following every move that I made.

"Haven't you been to sleep?" I challenged.

She nodded, patting the wire-and-rubber contraption on the bed beside her.

"Bendy and I were dreaming."

This was one area in which I didn't care to be involved. Sophie's dreams are guaranteed to send an analyst to the bottle. I slipped into my pajamas, brushed my teeth, and cut the light. It was somehow easier to talk without her eyes on me.

"You remember those pictures they gave you at Canada House — the ones with the mountains and snow?" Someone had presented her with a set of publicity stills. I heard her breathing as she does when she's concentrating heavily.

"You mean the ones with the bears?" she asked.

I'd forgotten about those. "No bears, sweetheart, but there's everything else. We're going there on vacation. You'll be able to build a snowman, ride on a sled, all sorts of exciting things."

There was a moment's silence, then the cot moved. "I'm not going to school, Papa."

I turned over on my side. There was enough light from the street for me to see her, clutching Bendy defensively. You'd have thought a kidnap attempt was to be made on the pair of them.

"Who said anything about school?" I demanded. "Why do you always have to be pessimistic? I said a vacation. Other little girls would be goddamned grateful if their papas bought them lots of new clothes."

"What color?" she asked immediately.

I groaned. "Who cares what color — blue — green — anything you want. Did you go to the john?"

Her voice was cutting. "Of course I did."

"Then go to sleep."

She managed it in two and a half minutes. She still sucks her thumb in moments of supreme contentment, effectively sealing her mouth. The outcome is that she breathes with a snuffling sound that you simply have to learn to live with. I do this by using two pillows. One is pinned under my head, the other clamped over the upturned ear. The snuffling still filters through but only faintly. Right now the noise was a good omen that she'd accepted the idea of the trip. With luck the rest would be taken in stride. I cat-napped all night, waking and looking across at the dresser. Each time the pile of money made a reassuring sight.

Chapter Two

THE SOUND of running water told me that it was morning. There was no need to check my watch for the exact hour. If Sophie was up it was half after seven. It was a gray day beyond the windows but at least it was dry. The pigeons that infested the block were scuffling about on the window ledges. I forced myself out of bed and went into the kitchen. Sophie was setting the table for breakfast. I never let her mess with the stove, but apart from that she can prepare a simple meal as well as any woman I've ever known. And she's a lot more restrained verbally.

I did a few painful push-ups as Sophie watched me through the bathroom door. It's a difficult enough performance without having a critical audience. I kicked the door shut. By the time I had shaved, toast was waiting for me. I kissed her, put the coffeepot on the burner and two eggs to boil. Then I inspected her ears and her nails. They were impeccable.

"Terrific," I said. "See if you can remember to deal with your knees at the same time in future."

She turned the egg timer upside down and watched the sand trickle.

"You snored," she remarked after a while.

After the Scotch I'd drunk the night before I was well able to believe it. I decapitated the eggs and changed the subject.

"You're going out shopping with Joan, honey. You'll like that, won't you — lots of new things to wear?"

She licked the back of her spoon, eying me the while craftily.

"Do I get to go to the Toy Fair?"

"You do not," I said firmly. "Christmas has gone and there'll be no time for visits to toy fairs. And while we're talking about it, you'd better choose which doll you're going to take with you. There can only be one, remember."

She glanced at the wired rubber contraption beside her. Most of the colors had been licked or worn off and the head sagged sadly.

"Bendy isn't a doll, stupid."

I'm too wise to be caught in that sort of trap now. "You watch your language," I warned. "If you're through eating, wipe your face, and don't hang around in the bathroom. There are things to be done."

It was half-past eight when the phone rang. Crying Eddie's voice was curt.

"The Ritz at two, O. K.?"

He waited just long enough to hear my acknowledgment and hung up smartly. I can remember thinking that if it hadn't been for Chalice the last place Eddie would have been heading for was Switzerland. His tastes were obstinately insular. I opened the closet door. The two vuition bags on the shelf above were relics of palmier days. Sophie watched me start to pack, leaning against the wall and picking her nose. Most of the stuff I was taking hadn't been used for years, clothes I'd brought over from Canada. Checked flannel shirts, warm long johns, a pair of earmuffs. I'd no idea what a prairie-province mining magnate was supposed to wear, but I packed my dinner jacket.

I dressed Sophie in her duffle coat, made sure that her legs were protected, and took her downstairs to the girls' apartment. Joan was running a Hoover over the carpet, a cigarette stuck in the side of her mouth, a kitchen cloth tied over her ratty hair like a headscarf. Her roommate had already gone to work. There aren't too many secrets in the apartment building. People tend to live their lives and the hell with what the neighbors think. The Scribners are the exception. I told Joan what I wanted her to buy for Sophie. She heard the news with frank disbelief.

"*Ski clothes for Switzerland!* You're putting me on, dasher, you must be!"

"Peasant," I said. "Don't you know it's what the idle rich always do at this time of the year? Keep five of this for beer. I don't care if you spend the rest, just have Sophie back here by noon."

She counted the bills mechanically before stuffing them into her jeans.

"Sixty-five quid! You rob a bank or something, Henderson?"

I sat Sophie down on the sofa. "You're a coarse woman and I wonder why I put up with you. Make sure you look after my child in the proper manner."

The rental office in the lobby was open. The clerk had his feet up on the desk and was drinking tea from a saucer. He was wearing a shiny-elbowed jacket and the beard from the previous day. The two-bar heater behind was dangerously near his buttocks. His breath stank of pickled onions. All in all, he was a dismal sight.

"I know," he said wearily. "Eight-C's making too much noise, or is it the drains again?"

I reached inside my jacket and gave him a brief show of the roll. I peeled a pound note off and let it drift down to the desk in front of him. He assumed a stunned expression.

"Buy yourself a drink," I said airily. "We'll be away for a few days. See that my account's ready for me when I return. There *was* something I wanted to complain about, come to think of it. Try to have the Scribners keep their dog under control. The corridor's a disgrace."

He was on his feet, bowing. "I'll see to it myself, Mr. Henderson. And you and the baby have a good trip, sir."

I called a Chelsea number from the booth in the lobby. A man's voice answered immediately. The vowels were Canadian, the rest of the voice detribalized.

"Gordon Campbell speaking. Good morning!"

"Paul Henderson," I announced. "When could I see you, Gordy?"

"That depends," he stalled. "How long would you need?"

"Half an hour at the outside."

I heard the radio playing in the background. They'd be sitting in the breakfast annex, the river at their feet beyond the window. Gordy would have mouthed my name and Alison's lips would be thin with distaste.

"I'll be at the office at nine-fifteen," he said. "Is that any good to you?"

"I'll see you there," I answered, and hung up. Gordy Campbell and I had been at school together. His father, like mine, was a United Empire Loyalist and a militant Anglophile. Some of all this had rubbed off on Gordy. He'd opted for Oxford in preference to McGill and taken an honors degree. That much was fairly predictable; what came next wasn't. Gordy had married a don's daughter and studied law. Eleven years later he was a partner in one of the best criminal-law offices in town.

King's Road was the usual crawl of snarled traffic and bus convoys. I walked west toward the post office. It was too early for the freak parade, another half-hour before the street was hideous with music spewing from the tatty boutiques.

The post office was empty save for a man in a cloth cap drawing his old-age pension. I sent off a cable to the Palace Hotel, Todtsee.

RESERVE SUITE AND ACCOMMODATION FOR TWO SERVANTS FOR TWO WEEKS STOP ARRIVING TOMORROW STOP PAUL HENDERSON

It was a gambit that had been successful in the past. Whether or not it would get us into the Palace Hotel remained to be seen.

The clerk's pencil skipped over the words and there was a shadow of envy in his voice.

"Did you want this to go night-letter rate or ordinary rate?"

My morale had taken too much of a beating over the past year or so. I couldn't help the satisfaction in my own voice.

"The quickest way possible, please."

Gordy Campbell's offices are in a building that faces Trafalgar Square and no more than a hundred yards from Canada House. It's maybe twice that distance to Piccadilly Circus and close to the Law Courts. It might help describe the sort of guy Gordy is if I say that five nights a week, rain or shine, he walks home to Chelsea — through Saint James's Park, along Buckingham Palace Road, and then south to the Embankment. He buys his afternoon paper from the same man, slips a guy in a wheelchair a weekly handout, and leaves his job in his office.

I left the elevator at the tenth floor, turned right, and walked along a well-remembered corridor. The suite is the last one on the west side of the building. There are three solid-looking doors. One says PRIVATE, a second CAMPBELL & KLINE, SOLRS & COMMISSIONERS FOR OATHS, the third is unmarked. This is the one I used, bypassing the waiting room and appearing directly in the outer office. The same two girls were there. Alice-in-Wonderland on the switchboard and the redhead from Halifax, Nova Scotia. I fluttered my fingers at each in turn.

"Hi, Sue — hi, Marge!"

Marge leaned her elbows on the desk and frowned. "Well, just look who we've got here! If it isn't Bonnie Prince Charlie himself. Good morning, sir, and what may we do for you?"

I reached over, took her freckled nose between my finger and thumb, and tweaked it gently.

"You can show a little respect for a start. Is anyone in?"

"Mr. Campbell, and he's waiting for you. Go through."

Both these kids had been good to me when I needed it. There'd been a gap of a week before Gordy had managed to get bail for me. The night I went to Brixton Prison, Marge had taken Sophie home with her. For the next six days, she and Sue had managed my daughter between them. Gordy's wife had refused to have the kid in her house.

I opened Gordy's door. He was on his feet before I reached the big leather-topped desk. He doesn't look like a lawyer. He's six-three with the build of the good hockey player he used to be. He was wearing a double-breasted check suit with a carnation in the lapel. His hair is the color of rusty iron and inclined to curl. He punched me lightly on the bicep and sat me down where he could see me.

"You son of a gun," he said finally. "Why haven't you been near me in all this while?"

We were sitting at a level with Nelson's statue. The wheeling pigeons were almost imperceptible against the gray sky.

"Come off it," I said. "You know why well enough. I owe you money."

He shook his head. His forehead and cheeks were still tanned from a Bermuda sun.

"That sounds like one hell of a lousy reason from a guy I went to school with. I told you at the time, that Old Bailey thing was on the house. Call it a thank-you for all those summers up at Lake Wasaga — call it anything you like, but don't talk to me about owing money. You paid the barrister anyway."

I shrugged. "You'll get paid, Gordy. Listen, what would you say if I told you I was about to come into a fortune — an enormous sum of money?"

"You kidding?" he asked.

I shook my head. His face was suddenly serious. He started rolling a gold pencil to and fro across the blotter. Then he looked up.

"Are you asking me as a friend or a lawyer?"

"I'm asking you as a lawyer."

His eyes lost their usual hint of laughter. "I'd say supply

nothing but your name and address and hold tight till I get there."

There was an awkward silence and then we both grinned. "What the hell are you getting yourself into now?" he demanded. "I've told you a dozen times to let me look around for something for you. There are plenty of people who could use a guy like you."

He meant what he said. That was the saddest thing about it. He still saw me as the hockey hero who'd been caught smoking in the locker room. We'd been too close for his wife's dislike to come between us. But there was nothing he could do for me and well I knew it. I kept my voice level, trying to stop the bitterness from creeping into my answer.

"Do we have to go through all this again, Gordy? You know I couldn't get a job as a men's-room attendant. They're probably choosy about character references. Let's drop the subject."

He held up both hands, palms facing me. "O.K., O.K. How's Sophie?"

"Sophie is great," I answered. "She and I are going on a little trip. Yours not to reason why. What I need from you is a deed of trust made out in her favor — something that can't possibly be broken. In a week's time you'll have the funds to put into it. And don't capsize when you see the figures on the check."

The pencil came to rest in his fingers. Gordy's never asked more than the minimal necessary questions.

"You want me to take care of this personally? I mean is there any reason Jake Klein shouldn't know about it? Deeds of trust aren't really my line of country."

"Look," I said. "I don't give a goddamn who does the thing as long as it's burglar-proof."

42

His half-smile was completely without malice. "There's no trust that a smart lawyer can't break, given enough time and money. You ought to know that, Paul."

I took the shot without anger. "O.K. Let's just try to make the thing a whole lot tighter than my grandmother's lawyer did."

He touched a buzzer and Marge came in with a pad. He gave her a few necessary details — the place and time of Sophie's birth, the objects of the deed of trust, and the length of time it would have to run.

"Get Mr. Klein to look this over. Tell him it's for Mr. Henderson."

I stood up. "I'll see you in about a week's time, Gordy."

He just nodded and gave me his hand. "I don't want to know a damn thing, Paul. Just take care of yourself and think of Sophie."

"I already have," I answered. "Take it easy."

I left his office, as always the better for seeing him. It was ten by now and my next port of call was a bookstore on Old Brompton Road. I paid off the cab at South Kensington Station, walked through one exit and out the other. The mechanics of evasion become habit over the years. You do this sort of thing automatically. I was thinking about the coming interview.

If you live in a city the size of London, there is one certainty you can bet on. Somewhere, not too far away, fugitives from the law will be holed up in a back-street hotel, a suburban roominghouse, or a trusted friend's cellar. They'll have run as far and as hard as they can. And the net is closing in on them. Neighborhood cops are knocking on doors. Descriptions are being flashed onto television screens. The stool pigeons are sidling in and out of the fugitives' known haunts. A guy in a spot like this has only one hope — he has to get hold of a false passport and make a dash for a boat or a plane. Most of them are amateur criminals. Defaulting bank clerks, the guy who's just buried his wife in the back yard. And the business of procuring false passports is strictly in the hands of the pros.

The pros are careful who they deal with. There are no workshops with presses banging out the blue, gold-embossed tickets to freedom. In peacetime anyway, the bottle-nosed ex-major who eases up in the saloon bar with a winey whisper about a pal in the passport office is no more than he appears to be — a cheap false-pretender. If the law is after you and you want out of the country, there are only three ways of doing it: you stow away, with or without help; you make an application for a passport, supplying false particulars; or you go to someone like Monkey Farrell.

Farrell's formula is a simple play on credulity. Now and again he walks into an employment agency with a yarn about looking for staff. He varies the age and occupation of his prospective employee. It could be a salesman, a clerk, or a chauffeur. The one common factor is that these men must be prepared to travel. The salary Farrell offers is a generous one, and the line forms on the right. The first question he asks is whether his man already has a passport. If the answer is yes, he gets rid of the guy immediately and passes on to the next.

This chap has never been out of the country. Right, says Farrell, and whips out a passport application form. These he picks up by the dozen in travel agencies. He tells the guy to fill it in, to have his picture taken and authenticated by some reputable British citizen — someone who has known the applicant over the years and who will vouch for him. When that's done, says Farrell, bring the whole lot back to me and I'll take care of everything. The mark leaves on a cloud. He's setting up house by now, in sun-drenched Australia or wherever. There's always someone who will vouch for him, a family friend, the doctor who brought him into the world. Ministers of the gospel are much in favor. Back comes the guy with the forms completed. Farrell claps him on the shoulder and sets a departure date.

A couple of days go by. Farrell gets in touch with the mark. They meet. Something's come up, Farrell explains regretfully. There's been a change in his plans and the whole project is shelved. I'm very sorry but keep in touch. Meanwhile, here's a fiver for your trouble. Now comes the legerdemain. He produces an application form and the guy's picture and tears them up in front of him. No sense, he says, in me paying for a passport you're not going to use. What he's really done is tear up a forged form. They part.

The beauty of this scheme lies in its simplicity. Farrell now has all the information he needs. He goes to Somerset House and buys a copy of the mark's birth certificate. The shift is that the photograph that will be sent to the passport office will be your photograph or mine. Farrell simply forges the original sponsor's name on the back. The copy of the birth certificate is merely added documentation. The passport office handles around seventy thousand requests a month. They can only employ spot checks.

We'll assume that a security officer picks a paper at random and flukes one of Farrell's productions. The officer's first call will be to the Registrar-General of Births, Deaths, and Marriages. "Was John Doe born at such a time and place?" He was. The next check is on the referee himself. We'll assume this one to be a clergyman. The officer looks him up in Crockford's Clerical Directory. The reverend's name, address, and telephone number are listed. The security officer calls the number and identifies himself. "Have you recently sponsored a passport application for Mr. John Doe? You have . . . then do you know the applicant personally?" He does indeed; he's known him since he was a lad. In fact, he baptized him. End of security check. Neither the officer nor the clergyman knows that the picture about to be pasted into the passport is yours or mine and not John Doe's. The passport is mailed to a drop address, where Farrell collects it.

The nickname, Monkey, stems from one of Farrell's idiosyncracies, an excess of cunning. He's incapable of volunteering information of any kind. He treats a simple inquiry about the weather as he would an attempt to ascertain his bank balance. The story goes that he flushes the john three times to make sure. True or not, it's a measure of his caution. The con mob use him frequently. Visiting Australians working the boats stock up with two or three passports to see them through the trip home. The only business I had ever done with Farrell had been the previous year. It was part of my deal with that swell Cody that I was to provide with a phony p.p. Luckily enough, he'd never known where it was supposed to come from — nor had it been delivered. Chalice's choice of Farrell was another indication that he was hiring nothing but the best.

The faded sign hanging over the store on the corner of Hollywood Road proclaimed

ALOYSIUS FARRELL
OLD BOOKS AND PRINTS

A bell tinkled as I pushed the door open. The long narrow room had the acid smell of print and mildewed leather. The shelves on the walls were crammed with the works of long-forgotten authors. Rolled-up prints littered the tables like samples of wallpaper. A gas heater was spluttering in front of a bowl of water. An empty cup and saucer stood on the wicker chair beside it. A fly-spotted painting hung near a door at the far end of the room. The subject was death in the jungle, a lion surrounded by noble savages. I addressed my voice at the holes bored in the painting and the wall behind.

"Good morning, sir. I represent the Chelsea Chamber of Commerce. We've been getting complaints about the quality of the merchandise you're selling here."

A door opened slowly on a tall, stooped man dressed in stained corduroy slacks and a moth-eaten sweater hanging down to his knees. He looked as if he'd been stretched on a rack. I heard the bones in his elbow click as he passed a hand over his pallid bald pate. The other hand was holding a dirty typed card that had obviously been used and used again. The message on it read: *Back in half an hour or thereabouts.*

He hung the card in the window, pulled down a blind, and locked the street door. I followed him into what he called his office. Books were piled from the floor to the ceiling. There was just enough space to edge through sideways to the old-fashioned desk. The typewriter on it looked as old as its owner. He peered through the holes in the wall and sat down with his hands on his knees. His Dublin accent was gratingly genuine.

"You know me rules, Henderson. Money first. A hundred and fifty nicker."

I cleared a space on the ripped leather sofa. If the law ever arrived with a search warrant, it would take them a month to search the place.

"That's seventy-five quid each, you old goat," I challenged. "A year ago it was fifty."

Dried fragments of dyspepsia tablets crusted the corners of his mouth. He nodded a couple of times evilly.

"Old goat, is it? Well, the back of me hand to you, you Canadian good-for-nothing. Let's see the money."

I gave it to him. He checked each bill, holding it up in front of the lamp and looking at the watermark. Finally he stuffed the roll in his filthy pants and smiled. The maneuver revealed a mouthful of National Health Service teeth, each tooth a perfect match for its neighbor. It was like seeing a corpse with a young man's smile. He gave me a key with a number on the shank.

"You'll find the goods at Victoria Station. That'll be another four bob for the key."

I shook my head dumbly and found the coins. He swung around and started scratching out a receipt for thirty shillings. This too was part of his mystique. Every visitor had to have a legitimate reason for calling at the bookshop. The receipt he handed me looked as if a spider had paddled in ink and walked across the paper. He selected a fly-spotted print at random from a pile behind him, rolled it up, and gave it to me, still grinning.

"You're the proud owner of a work of art the likes of which has never been surpassed. A genuine Foley it is, depicting the immortal Tolpuddle martyrs on their way to the pokey. Now get out of me shop, and may good luck be always in front of ye."

He surveyed the street thoroughly before letting me out of

the door. I dropped the print and receipt in the first trash can I saw and walked to the line of taxis outside South Kensington subway. Victoria Station is no place to loiter. The whizz mob works the boat trains, relieving simpletons of their vacation money. Cheap hookers use the bars. Dropouts hang around, sleep in the waiting rooms, and take trips in the lavatories. All this attracts the law. While I was technically clean, I was in no mood for an interview with some hard-nosed cop playing a hunch.

Farrell's choice of locker was typical. It was the last one in the row, a couple of steps away from the badly lighted booking hall. He'd be able to flit from one to the other unnoticed. God knows what sort of precautions he took on occasions like these. He probably wore a cloak and a wide slouch hat. The passports were in a plain brown envelope. I left the scene by the Buckingham Palace Road exit, grabbed another cab, and examined the envelope. Farrell had given us our money's worth. Both passports had the appearance of use. Each bore a couple of exit and entrance stamps. Chalice's name was Harold Crane. Crying Eddie was Edward Thomas. Mr. Crane and Mr. Thomas. I couldn't help grinning.

Most law-abiding citizens think of thieves as slit-mouthed, humorless villains. It's not necessarily true. I'd been involved in a dozen capers that I could never have endured without a sense of humor. For instance, you spend a month casing a place. You go to the same restaurants as your prospective victim, catalogue her jewelry from a nearby table. Comes the night of the hit. Everything has been taken care of. The car has been parked safely out of sight. You make your sneak entrance into the block. You tiptoe along the corridor, insert the skeleton key, and gently turn it. The door is now open. Suddenly you hear a completely strange voice inquiring, "Is that you, Edith?"

And you get out of there in a hurry. It turns out that you're in the right building but on the wrong floor. The fact that the same skeleton key fitted both locks is pure coincidence. I don't claim that you're actually laughing as you run, but you get around to it later. The more I thought about Chalice and Eddie as Mr. Crane and Mr. Thomas, the surer I was that there'd be some comical angles to the caper before we were through.

I bought myself a beaver hat in a store on Piccadilly, a silky dark brown affair that the salesman claimed gave me an air of distinction. It matched the lining of my overcoat, anyway. The offices of Chiltern Air Charter were on the second story of a building facing Albemarle Street post office. I poked my head into a well-lit room furnished with chrome chairs and tables. There was a big display of aerial photographs, magazines connected with all aspects of flying. A young guy in his shirt sleeves and wearing a Robin Hood haircut glanced up from his desk. His heavy-framed spectacles gave him a severely studious look.

"Good morning, sir. What can I do for you?"

The room was overheated with potted plants pushing greenery in every direction. I took off my hat and coat and sat down opposite him.

"I want to charter a plane. I have to meet some business associates in Switzerland, but our schedule isn't firm yet."

He was square-jawed and the eyes behind the spectacles looked intelligent. His inspection of me was thorough without appearing discourteous.

"May I have your name, sir?"

"Paul Henderson," I replied.

He wrote on a pad. "And the address?"

I waved a hand. "I'm leaving the country by car this afternoon. You'd better make that in care of Canada House. It will always reach me."

He made another annotation. "I don't want to sound stupid, Mr. Henderson, but wouldn't a Swiss company be better for you?"

"I don't think so," I said easily. "Otherwise I'd be using one. There's the question of communications. I only speak English and my plane may entail a couple of quick trips back to England. The main thing is to have the plane at base. For the moment, the base is Todtsee in the Engadine."

"I'm familiar with Todtsee," he answered. He pulled a book from a rack and consulted it. "That would be all right, sir. They've extended the runways. What sort of plane did you have in mind, Mr. Henderson?"

I gave him an affluent smile. "I thought you'd tell me. We'll be four at least, possibly six."

He seemed to make up his mind about me. I had a feeling that he'd had to deal with cranks in his time and had just crossed me off the list.

"How long would the charter be for, sir?"

"A week, starting from tomorrow. I'll let you know in good time if it needs to be extended."

He flipped a folder over the desk. Inside was a set of pictures showing a good-looking plane in various stages of flight.

"Our flagship," he said. "A Beechcraft King Air 100. This airplane is a pressurized propjet and carries eight passengers in the utmost comfort. Cruising speed is two hundred eighty-five miles per hour. Charter cost is one hundred fifty pounds per day, payable in advance. This includes landing fees. The pilot's expenses are your charge as well as the fuel costs. If you want a stewardess that can be arranged."

"A stewardess won't be necessary." I gave him back the folder. "That seems O.K. I'll leave a couple of hundred pounds as deposit and send the rest around this afternoon. I want the plane in Todtsee by tomorrow evening."

He typed out a contract and gave me a receipt for the money.

"Your pilot's name is Captain Baxter, Mr. Henderson. Do you have an address in Todtsee where he can contact you?"

"The Palace Hotel, but I'll contact him. I imagine he stays around the airfield most of the time?"

He nodded earnestly. "The plane is yours for the period of charter, Mr. Henderson. Captain Baxter will be at your disposal night and day. You'll find him an easy man to get along with — he's South African. That reminds me, what is your nationality? We have to state the nationality of the hirer."

I put on my topcoat. "I'm Canadian. You'll have your money before three o'clock. Mail the receipt to me in care of Canada House."

I walked across the street and called Chalice from the post office. My message was garbled but he caught on and promised to have the cash sent around to the charter company by special messenger. I took a cab home. My entrance into the apartment building was marked by a whole series of double takes. It was either the beaver hat or the news of my sudden affluence.

The guy from the liquor store stood in his doorway, wagging his head in silent admiration. I could do no more than pay his bill before going up to the Australian girls' flat. Joan was with Sophie in the living room. The whole place was knee-deep in boxes and wrapping paper. Sophie greeted me, screaming with excitement and hopping from one foot to the other.

"Look, Papa, *look!*"

She paraded around, modeling a shorn-lamb coat with a bucket hood, fur-lined boots, and a minute pair of ski pants. I covered my ears with my hands and shouted.

"*Quiet!* goddamn it! Will you please quit screaming and be quiet!"

Joan gave me a wry grin. "I did what you said and spent out. There's no change coming. The bills are on the table."

I looked at them mechanically. It's no trick to spend sixty-five pounds on a seven-year-old if you choose the right place. I grabbed Sophie by the hand and collected an armful of the new clothes. Joan carried the rest to the elevator. Upstairs I fixed something to eat and ordered transport for half after one. It took me twenty minutes and the threat of a beating to get Sophie out of her new ski pants. The clothes Joan had bought were expensive but warm and attractive. There was even a party dress of dark blue velvet with a matching hair band. I packed the gear into Sophie's bag, closed all the windows, and left notes for the people who brought the bread and milk.

I left the apartment by the back door. Two flights of service stairs took me up to the roof. It looked as if no one had been up there since V-E Day. Refuse was trapped at the base of the parapet. Rain and sun had processed wads of paper into weird art forms. Inches of greasy soot lay in the sheltered places. I unlocked the weather-beaten storage shed. There was little inside. A couple of faded deck chairs, some odds and ends of wire netting, a length of rubber hose. The one window in the ceiling was covered with bird lime. I lifted the oilskin pouch from its hiding place. It had lain there since the night of my arrest. I pulled out its contents. A coat of Vaseline protected the picklocks and the two rings of skeleton keys. There was a pair of forceps for turning a key from the outside. I put the tool kit in my pocket and went downstairs.

Sophie was scuffing up the toes of her new boots against the table leg. I sat her down on the sofa.

"Let's you and I have a little talk," I said. "I want you to behave yourself on this trip, do you hear? I want you to say please and thank you and curtsy without falling on your can. O.K.?"

Joan had brushed Sophie's hair to a pale gold cap and fastened it with a slide.

"I've been good all morning," she said. There was a slight hesitation. "What's a mite, Papa?"

"A *what?*" I demanded incredulously. "What do you get these words from, anyway?"

"From Mrs. Scribner." She cocked her head. "Me and Joan heard her as we came in. 'Poor little mite,' she said."

I could imagine the look of disapproval that would have accompanied the remark. Nobody was better at a public hatchet job than Lavinia Scribner.

"She must have been talking about her husband," I said. "Let's go back to square one. Remember what I told you in Spain — if you're lost, you go straight to a policeman. What's your name when people ask you, honey?"

"Sophia Matilda Henderson. I'm seven years old and we're Canadians. My father . . ."

"That's enough," I said. "You don't talk to strange men and you blow your nose on your handkerchief."

She sat down and we waited for the cab to arrive. The phone rang and we went downstairs. The manager of the liquor store wished us a pleasant journey. There was nobody else in the lobby to see our departure. The driver took the short way through St. James's Park. Mounds of dirty snow lay beneath skeletal trees. The sky overhead was the color of pewter. A few people were striding about determinedly, but the only living things that looked contented were the Muscovy ducks. The cab stopped in front of the Arlington Street entrance. I left the bags with the doorman, explaining that a car would be calling for me. Sophie entered the Ritz as if it were her second home.

It was five minutes to two when Chalice appeared, dressed in striped pants, a black overcoat, and carrying a bowler hat. He walked across the lobby, holding his head with a peculiar stiffness. He looked like a funeral mute as much as anything. As he came closer I saw what was wrong with him. His neck was trapped in a high, starched collar. He came to a dead halt in front of us, and for one horrified moment I thought he was going to salute. He seemed to catch himself just in time. He blinked rapidly, careful with his aspirate.

"I have the Rolls-Royce outside, sir."

I widened my smile, speaking under my breath. "Let's not overdo it."

He took the bags from the porter and stowed them in the magnificent car parked at the bottom of the steps. Looking at its gleaming perfection, you could believe the boasts about the seventeen coats of paint and all the rest of it. Crying Eddie was upright behind the wheel, gloved fingers tapping impatiently. The only sour note was the rakish angle of his cap. Chalice took the seat beside him. Sophie climbed in back with me. The dividing glass disappeared at the touch of a button. I leaned forward and tapped Eddie on the shoulder.

"O.K., Macarthur, let's have the cap on straight, shall we?"

His eye met mine in the driving mirror. He corrected the angle with a grimace.

"Certainly, sir."

The envelope Chalice handed me contained the car documents and tickets, a train voucher to ferry the car from Zürich to Todtsee. The Rolls crossed Westminster Bridge. The sensation was like traveling in a jet plane but without the screaming noise of the engines. Sophie had propped Bendy on the seat beside her and was bouncing up and down trying all the buttons on the control board.

Crying was an expert driver, about the best wheelman in the business. His escapes from the law, traveling at a hundred miles an hour, are referred to as classics. Right now he kept his speed just below those shown on the signs along the highway. Chalice rubbed the back of his neck. An angry red line had appeared there.

"I'll have to get rid of this fucking thing," he said with feeling. He swung around, eyes penitent, a hand covering his mouth. "I'm sorry, mate."

But Sophie hadn't even heard. She was staring at Crying Eddie's head, fascinated.

"That man just wiggled his ears, Papa. Make him do it again!"

The skin on Eddie's neck flushed but he maintained a dignified silence.

"Wiggle your ears, Ed," Chalice ordered.

Sophie giggled and I looked away hurriedly. When I faced front again, Eddie had put on a pair of dark glasses that gave him a highly sinister appearance.

"I can see this is going to be a doddle," he said bitterly. "I can see that already. My old mum was right; I ought to have my head examined."

"Your old mum ain't never been right," answered Chalice. "Anyway, not since she had you. Put your brakes on and stop this bleedin' motorcar."

The Rolls came to a smooth halt. Chalice turned around in his seat, grinning like a fox.

"I bet the little girl'd like to ride in front with Eddie, wouldn't she?"

I barely moved my head and she was over the seat in a flash. Chalice took her place and wound up the dividing partition. We were out on the motorway by now, traveling with a new surge of power, the countryside flicking past us. Chalice inspected both passports minutely. I could see his lips working as he memorized the names. He put them away in his pocket.

"That old bastard does a good job, whatever you say about him. Are you keeping an account of what you spend?"

I nodded. "I'll soon be out of cash. You said the best, and the best costs money."

He lifted a shoulder easily and lit a cheroot. "We'll take care of it as soon as we get to Zürich. Just don't say nothing to Eddie about how much you're spending. He's liable to stop sleeping."

I lit a smoke of my own. We were rushing past flooded fields sad with sodden hayricks. But it was warm in the back of the car and the loudest sound was the hiss of the tires.

"Do you mind if I ask you something again, Harry? It's been on my mind. Are you one hundred per cent sure that this gas will really put people out for as long as two hours? All it needs is for just one of those jokers to come around before that and we've had it. Our whole plan's being built on the premise that we'll have enough time to get out of Switzerland before the whistle blows."

He drew hard on the cheroot till the end glowed. He waited for the ash to cool before he answered.

"Look, Paul, there are certain things you and me's got to take on trust about one another. You say you can case Bergen's house without anyone being the wiser. I accept that. If I say two hours minimum it's because I *know*, mate. I don't risk me neck or me cash without making sure of the facts."

There was a certain air about him at moments like this that, had he said he could walk on water, I'd have probably believed him.

"O.K.," I said hurriedly. "With the plane we've got, we can be in Antwerp in two hours. Antwerp's where my buyer is." We'd never spoken again about Van der Pouk since that first time, and my voice sounded a little strained.

He fingered the back of his neck tenderly. "I can't go on wearing these bleedin' things, that's for sure. Wouldn't I be all right in soft collars?"

"Sure," I said. "You realize I'll have to make delivery of the loot myself. I told you, my man doesn't do business with third parties."

"You told me," he said. If my voice was strained, his was completely relaxed.

"Maybe it doesn't worry you," I insisted. "But what about Eddie?"

He pitched his cheroot butt through the window. "You worry too much about Eddie. You ever read anything about Field Marshal Rommel?"

I made a gesture of dissent. "I never read war stories. It's a subject that bores me."

"Then it shouldn't," he said softly. "Because you're at war right now, mate. The Desert Fox, they used to call him. They seek him here and they seek him there. All that Montgomery's lot would be after him and old Rommel would vanish in a dust storm. That's the kind of general I'd have been." His dark eyes shone with enthusiasm.

"I guess you would," I answered. "Trouble is you never got past corporal."

We reached Lydd Airport forty-five minutes later. There was a quarter-hour wait, during which Sophie took possession of the lounge. She bought herself a Coke at the bar, poked her nose into half a dozen offices, wandered into passport control. Our flight was finally called. Our bags had been left in the Rolls. The only thing to fear was some sort of currency check. The fact that I had a Canadian passport helped. I answered a few routine questions truthfully. Chalice and Crying Eddie sat shoulder to shoulder in the departure lounge. One would have had to know them well to detect the wary flicker in their eyes, the way Chalice kept blocking a yawn. I knew why they were nervous. They were used to going into action for no more than a few explosive seconds, their heads shrouded in silk stockings.

I watched the Rolls driven into the belly of the squat Bristol. Nobody else had been called for the flight. Ours was the only car aboard. A few minutes later a door behind us opened. The faintly haughty voice belonged to a blond stewardess.

"May I have your attention, please. Will you follow me now and no smoking till the aircraft has taken off." She took Sophie's hand and walked across the tarmac, moving as if her legs were fastened together at the knees.

Going through a frontier post is a strain on the nerves. The minutes drag and you wonder if you're ever going to make it. Cops come and go. Hatches are raised. Eyes inspect you through the slits. The worst of all is the bell that rings suddenly. You're dead sure that it's a prelude to your arrest.

I climbed onto the plane with a feeling of profound relief. We rolled to the end of the runway and the stubby wings shuddered. The noise of the motors was suddenly deafening. There was a rush of wind, and we were airborne, climbing and banking steeply. Sheep dotted the marshland below. England slipped away behind chalk cliffs. The boats in the Channel below appeared motionless. Then we were above cloud and into sunshine.

We reached Troyes in the late afternoon, a gray town where our stay was less than memorable. We checked into an hotel featuring fake beams and hostile personnel. I left Sophie in the room, walked downtown, and called an Antwerp number. It took me five minutes to work my way up to one of Van der Pouk's personal assistants. Van der Pouk himself was in New York but was expected back in two days' time. I left a message to the effect that Mr. Maple from London would be in Belgium the following week. There was no sign of Sophie when I returned, and I located her shrill treble somewhere along the corridor. I tracked her down to my partners' room. Chalice had gone out to buy soft collars. Sophie was sitting on the bed, listening to an improbable account of Crying Eddie's days as a sea scout.

I ran a bath and lay in it soaking. I was trying to re-create a picture of Shahpur in my mind. The nearer we came to Todtsee, the more conscious I was of the weight I was carrying. The job was as clear-cut as any I'd been on, in the sense that we knew exactly what we were going for. A hundred women would be cooped up in a ballroom and wearing some of the finest jewelry in the world. I no longer had any doubts about the gas and the plane would give us a perfect getaway. It was the period in between that was giving me trouble. To use the gas I had to get inside the house and Shahpur would be well protected against all possible assaults. The architect's drawings were bones without flesh. I had to know how many servants there were, the pattern of their behavior. All this was necessary to the mechanics of the hit, and we had little enough time to find these things out. There were no more than five days to Marika Bergen's gala. What I'd said to Chalice had been no boast. I'd hit too many places in my life not to be sure of myself. I could leave a house with no more trace of my visit than if a ghost had turned burglar. But what I could do was one thing. Whether I still had the nerve to do it was another.

Chapter Three

We checked out after an early breakfast and were in Basel by six in the evening. Another hour and a half saw us in Zürich. A cold damp fog shrouded the lake. There was less snow in the streets than in London. Our hotel was high on a hill near the zoo and full of Americans wearing natural-shoulder suits and smelling of toilet water. It seemed that there was some form of convention going on and they hunted one another through the public rooms, their eyes glinting behind spectacles as they cornered their prey.

Our suite had two bedrooms, carved-wood furniture, and some of the fiercest plumbing I had ever seen. The hot water jetted out like a geyser. It was eight o'clock when I ordered steaks to be sent up for Chalice, Crying, and Sophie. I left my daughter in bed, the others playing Chinese checkers, and went down to the bar. Zürich retires early. After one o'clock in the morning you might as well be in Lively, Ontario. I sat in the bar with a plate of smoked salmon and a bottle of Danish beer, warding off the flying champagne corks. The convention was breaking up. By the time the paper-hat and conga-chain stage was reached I'd had enough. Chalice called as I opened the door to the suite. He was sitting up in bed, dressed in black silk pajamas. He'd wrapped a towel around his sore neck and was reading a book with Rommel's picture on the cover. It was the classic picture, showing the German general standing in the cockpit of a tank, staring out across the desert. Crying Eddie was asleep in the other bed, hands crossed across his chest and snoring gently. He looked about as serene as a sleeping scorpion. Chalice held his place with a thumb and gestured at his partner with the other. He settled himself more comfortably.

"Don't pay no attention to him. You could drive a bleedin' bus through the room and he wouldn't wake up. Know what I've been thinking about, Paul? I've been thinking about this geezer in Antwerp — your buyer."

"What about him?" I removed Eddie's breeches from a chair and sat down.

Chalice turned the next page of his book as if he already knew what would be there, glanced at the text, and closed the covers.

"Well, in the first place, I don't see how any one man can handle that amount of loot."

"I can," I said, looking at the tray between their beds. There was very little left. Their appetites had been hearty. "If you've got the outlets that he has, there's no problem at all. We've been over all this before and you never complained."

"I'm not complaining," he said, opening his eyes. "We're having a friendly discussion without being bothered by Sleeping Beauty here. Does he know how much money's involved, this pal of yours?"

I leaned back in the chair, looking at him steadily. "We've

talked about that, too, Harry. You told me and I told him. Two hundred thousand pounds apiece which makes six hundred thousand in all."

"Maybe three hundred thousand apiece," he corrected. "Who can tell with them sort of people? I've been cataloguing the ones we know about and there's all the others. Me and Eddie's got bank accounts here in Zürich. That's where we want our money."

"You'll get it," I assured him. "The moment the gear's delivered, the cash will be on its way. Is that all or was there something else you wanted to see me about?"

I can remember a picture of one of the Stuart kings. A dark-faced saturnine character with a long upper lip. Chalice's features were cast in the same mold.

"That's all," he said, as though he was surprised at my asking. "I got a right to know what's going on, remember. I had to go to the baby, by the way. She was crying."

I was getting sick of hearing Sophie referred to as "the baby." She was seven years old.

"You sound like a broody hen," I said testily. "She was probably dreaming."

He shook his head. "I give her a drink of water. It makes you think, doesn't it? I seen a man's throat cut at her age."

The fact that it was probably true made the statement even more hideous. I got up from the chair.

"I've ordered breakfast for seven. The banks open at eight. Don't forget that you two are supposed to be dressed and ready for action by the time I get up. The train leaves Hauptbahnhof at three minutes after ten. O.K.?"

"O.K.," he said, and switched off the light.

There are three classic tests for a thief to prove his friend's loyalty. If he can confide either his woman or his money or

his liberty to an associate and come out of the experience un-
scathed he'll be doing well. A successful combination of two
of the factors is even better. A combination of all three is a
rarity. It marks the sort of relationship that breaks down
prison walls, defies physical and mental torture, and assumes
responsibility for a busted friend's family. There was no
woman involved in our case, but I went to sleep sure that
Chalice would pass the other two tests. We were at the bank
shortly after it opened in the morning. I went in with Chalice
while Sophie waited in the car with Crying Eddie. Chalice
cashed a check at a counter and handed me twenty-five hundred dollars in Swiss francs.

"Cop onto this, mate," he said. "And remember what I
told you. The best ain't good enough for us. Style, style,
and style — that's what this outfit's got to show. Just remember what you spend and how."

A loading crew put the Rolls onto a flatcar attached to the
Engadine Express. Everything went with Swiss precision.
It is rare that anything happens to spoil the image of their
absolute correctness. If somebody sticks up a bank, the as-
sailants turn out to be foreigners. It's foreigners who abuse
their political asylum. Foreigners create scandals and get
themselves trapped by avalanches. The Swiss treat each
happening on its merits with competence and a complete
lack of humor. Two things seem to blow their minds — an
invasion of their independence and assaults on property. I
had no illusions about police reaction to our plan. Anyone with Marika Bergen's kind of money was sacrosanct in
Switzerland. While the thought didn't worry me unduly, I
took it out occasionally, dusted it off, and considered the implications.

We boarded the train. Hundreds of skis were racked outside the coaches. Most of the passengers were bound for the thousand-meter slopes. Crying Eddie was getting plenty of attention from the sweater girls as we looked for our places. He gave no hint that he noticed it, clean-cut and handsome in his uniform, the suggestion of worry in his eyes adding to his interest. All he needed was a row of medal ribbons and he could have taken his place at a gathering of military attachés. He and Chalice vanished into second class to continue their marathon checker game. I put my hat and coat in the rack overhead and settled down behind the pages of the *Herald Tribune*. There was yet another piece on Bergen. An Englishwoman in the coach with us pounced on Sophie without knowing what she was getting into. In three minutes flat Sophie was displaying the quality of her underwear. It took her five more to explore that of her new-found friend. After an hour of it, the woman was wearing a slightly dazed expression. Her husband had long since taken refuge in the corridor, where he stood gloomily smoking a pipe.

The two powerful locomotives dragged the long train up through dripping and mist-shrouded forests. Lakes loomed out of the murk, dark green and uninviting. The narrow-gauge railroad tracks wound back on themselves in serpentine fashion. Half the train seemed to be permanently on view through the window. Every time we passed through one of the interminable tunnels, the skis racked on the outside of the coach rattled violently. Some kids down the corridor were drinking schnapps and singing. There was a sudden transformation outside. We came out of a tunnel to see silent stands of spruce, fir, and pine. There was snow everywhere — on the trees and across the valley to the mountains dominating it. We were in a realm of sunshine now, with woodsmoke curling in fat feathers over warm-looking farmhouses. Some children were hauling a sled over the frozen cart tracks. I could see oxen in a barn painted with figures of the Holy Family, a church with a roof like a gilded onion.

Sophie was drumming on the window, her feet in the woman's lap. I excused myself and the woman smiled weakly. I found Chalice's compartment. They were alone. I opened the door and sat down. Crying Eddie fanned the air violently.

"This is a nonsmoker, mate."

I stubbed out my butt. "Another half-hour and it'll all start happening. How do you feel?"

"All of a dither," Eddie said sarcastically. His eyes were like granite chips washed in a mountain stream.

Chalice put the checkerboard and pieces back in his bag. "It's like one of them travelogues — or a spy movie. I keep expecting Orson Welles to show up. Me and Ed's been talking, Paul. Once we're settled in the hotel, we're going to drive up to Bergen's place and give our eyes a chance. You know, like, to get the feel of things."

I dragged deep and blew the smoke at the moving floorboards. "Don't talk like a bubblehead. This woman's the biggest thing to hit Todtsee since the ski lift, Harry. I wouldn't be surprised if they put up a statue to her when she leaves. And there's one thing that's sure and certain. Anyone coming into town — any stranger — who shows interest in her isn't going to last long. And you guys want to drive around casing the joint! What do you think — the cops turn into morons the moment you're out of England?"

Crying Eddie spoke his piece with bitterness. "Out of

England! All I know about being out of England, mate, is that you can't get a decent cup of tea."

Chalice found the remark offensive for some reason, and exploded. *"Tea!* In fifty years' time all those old lags'll be shuffling round the exercise yards, talking about you — remembering the biggest jewel caper of all time — and here you are mumbling about tea. Why don't you belt up and listen to what Paul's saying?"

"Because I haven't heard him say anything worth listening to," Crying Eddie replied sulkily.

I knew I had to make a stand sooner or later. "Look, Harry, this clown's beginning to give me a bellyache. Tell him to ease off."

"That's right," Chalice frowned. "You're carrying on like a pair of slags! How do you think you'd have gone in the desert, sand in your nose and mouth, sand up your ass, and Rommel on your tail. Discipline and comradeship, that's what we needed then, mate."

Crying Eddie's mouth went thin. His voice was withering. *"You* needed? The nearest you got to the desert was a whorehouse in Naples, you and your bleedin' Rommel."

We pulled into Todtsee minutes later. The tracks were crowded. Spade-bearded men in tall fur hats kissed the hands of mysterious-looking women. Cops in gray-green uniforms moved among the disembarking passengers. Sophie was clinging to my hand, firing one question after another. We went to the back of the train, where the Rolls was already being unloaded. I distributed a handful of silver among the crew, noticing that a cop standing by had jotted down the car's registration number. The station barometer gave a reading of minus four degrees Centigrade. The glass was high and steady. We climbed in and Eddie took the wheel.

"Easy on the gas," I reminded. "And keep your foot off the brake pedal."

A sign outside in the station concourse pointed the way to the Palace Hotel. The narrow streets had been snowplowed and salted. Throngs jostled the sidewalks, heading for the lifts and cable cars that flashed on the distant sunlit slopes. Droshkies clip-clopped along, the passengers swathed in lap robes. Sophie's nose was pressed tight against the window. She was taking in everything. The black dots on the far-off *pistes* were skiers. Their descent left parallel tracks on the dazzling expanse of snow.

The Palace Hotel was a top-heavy building with ornately carved wooden balconies. A vast sun terrace behind led down to the frozen lake, where hooves had hammered the surface for thoroughbreds. Posters advertised the coming horse races. A *chasseur* steered us to a parking space on the hotel lot. Another man piled our bags onto a trolley. I adjusted my hat, took Sophie by the hand, and walked up the steps. Chalice and Crying Eddie were right behind us. The lobby was stifling. The smells were rich, and the sounds discreet — a quiet laugh, a distant bell, the tinkle of ice in a glass.

Most of the people sitting in the chairs were elderly Jews, bearing the look of the cultured and wealthy. They spoke to one another in relaxed voices, completely sure of themselves, as if confident that in Switzerland they were beyond insult or harassment. None of them as much as glanced at us as we crossed the lobby to the reception desk. The two clerks there were dressed in black and wore identical smiles of welcome. A man in a nearby chair lowered his magazine; his face was alert and watchful. Any cheap sneak thief would have recognized him as the house cop. I placed my passport on the counter.

"Paul Henderson. My reservations were made from London."

The two smiles faded immediately. "One moment, sir, if you please." They went into a huddle.

A third clerk rose in a stately way and came over carrying a cable form. He pitched his voice delicately, like a stranger telling you that a bird has fouled your hat.

"I'm afraid the hotel is completely booked, Mr. Henderson. We haven't a single vacancy till the third of March. I'm sorry."

We were speaking in English. Crying Eddie and Chalice were near enough to hear. I saw Chalice's jaw stiffen. I let go of Sophie's paw.

"There must be some mistake. You'd better check again. My secretary confirmed the booking by phone only yesterday afternoon."

He looked at me through his spectacles, his pose losing some of its loftiness.

"By *telephone*, sir? One minute, please." He riffled through some papers on the desk behind him and shook his head. "There's nothing here, I'm afraid, Mr. Henderson. Is it possible that your secretary might have made a mistake? Could it be one of the other hotels? I'll gladly check with them, if you wish."

I shooed Sophie over to Crying before she started asking about my secretary.

"I don't employ people who make mistakes. Tell the manager I'd like to see him."

70

All three men looked as if their pants had dropped. It took no more than a couple of minutes for me to be shown into a comfortable office overlooking the parking lot. A small man with a mustache greeted me urbanely.

"Dittler, Mr. Henderson. I understand there's some confusion about your booking."

The Rolls was parked directly underneath the window. I had a strong feeling that Mr. Dittler had been inspecting it. I bore down on him hard.

"This hotel was recommended to me by our ambassador. I don't make mistakes about names nor does my staff. What you choose to call confusion I call incompetence. I'd be glad to repeat that statement to your board of directors."

He gave himself a second to make up his mind about me. When he'd done so, he spoke as if through cotton and molasses.

"The whole thing is incomprehensible to me, Mr. Henderson. There has to be some sort of oversight, carelessness. I shall certainly make it my business to find out. The sad fact is that there isn't a single hotel room to be found in Todtsee. Most of the better accommodation was reserved months ago — for Miss Bergen's guests."

"Miss *Bergen*?" I repeated.

He bobbed his head, assessing me still further professionally. "Marika Bergen. She's taken a palace near here and is giving a ball there in a few days' time. It's a great honor for Todtsee. A number of very important people are staying as her guests. I would have thought you had read about it."

"I don't read the gossip columns," I said stiffly. I could hear Sophie's voice through the door. The sound gave me a sense of urgency. "What you're saying in fact is that because of this woman and the stupidity of your staff I'm being forced to leave Todtsee. I may not read the gossip columns, Mr. Dittler, but I can assure you that I'm quite capable of influencing their contents."

He held up a well-manicured hand. *"Please,* Mr. Henderson! I completely understand how you feel about this wretched business. How long had you thought of staying in Todtsee? A month, perhaps?"

I gave him back the same sort of smile so that we understood one another.

"I doubt if I'd stay as long but I'd be prepared to pay for a month."

His shift of stance brought him closer to me. "Then I think I can help you," he said quietly. "A nobleman who lives here occasionally rents his house to people of standing. I have to warn you that Prince Skomielna's thoughts about prices are fairly steep. It *is* high season, of course."

I nodded casually. "The price is no object. When could I see this house?"

He glanced at his watch. "The Prince is a late riser. It might be a little early, but I'll see if I can reach him." He dialed a number, smiling as he waited for an answer. I'd have hung up long before he did, but apparently he knew his party. He spoke rapidly in German and then cradled the phone.

"Prince Skomielna's compliments. He will be delighted if you will join him for breakfast. The *chasseur* will direct you to his house."

We shook hands and I joined the others again. No crystal ball was needed to know that Dittler would be onto a fat commission. The clerk with the spectacles leaned toward me, smiling apologetically. I opened the envelope he offered. The note inside was written on a piece of Swissair stationery.

To Mr. Paul Henderson Palace Hotel Todtsee 1020 hrs.
I am sleeping out at the airfield since there are no rooms
available in the town. A phone call or message to me here
will reach me in minutes. The plane has been refueled and I
await your instructions.

Burt Baxter

The *chasseur* loaded our bags in the car and directed me to
the Prince's house. Sophie turned the corners of her mouth
down.

"I want to stay here, Papa. Eddie said we would."

I opened the front door. "Get in and quit whining. Make
a right, Eddie, and keep going till you reach the ice stadium." I closed the glass partition, noticing that the manager
was at his window, watching our departure.

Chalice was sitting next to me, his bowler hat between his
legs. His dark face wore a worried look.

"I didn't like that at all, mate. On show with Old Bill sitting there clocking us."

I lit a cigarette and tried to calm him down. "You *saw*
him, didn't you? The time to start worrying is when you
don't see him."

His eyes lost some of their edginess. "At least that's
according to plan."

"I goofed there," I admitted. "I should have guessed
about the hotels. But as it is, it couldn't have turned out better. We've got a house. No waiters or chambermaids to gossip about us. Relax."

He grinned suddenly. "I'm going to have this bleedin' hat
stuffed when I get back to London. I'll give it to Doll to hang
in the club."

We drove through streets with overhanging wooden balconies, past a succession of jewelry stores and boutiques, a

snob-looking store that sold nothing but tea, coffee, and caviar. The way widened into an avenue of fat white trees where every other residence appeared to be a pension or *Fremdenheim*. HOUSE FULL signs hung in every entrance. The ice stadium was imposing enough in the sunshine with its flags. The parking lot was empty. Posters wrapped around the lamp standards displayed the attractions of the month.

INTERNATIONAL CURLING DERBY
HORSERACING ON SNOW
PALU DOWNHILL RACE
BOBSLED CHAMPIONSHIPS

The front gates and pay booths were shut. Another notice out front proclaimed

ALL FIXTURES IN THIS STADIUM ARE
CANCELED FOR THE MONTH OF JANUARY 1971

We drove past the Carlton Hotel and circled the students' village. The high banks of the international bobsled run appeared ahead. A crew of four were screaming down the icy tunnel at ninety miles an hour. The road ended abruptly at massive gates set in fieldstone walls.

"Open it," I said to Chalice.

He climbed out, the bowler hat low on his ears, and pushed an arm through the wrought iron. We drove into an enormous garden blanketed with snow. Statues of young men were dotted about, bending and stretching in the Greek tradition. The driveway rose to a commanding knoll. The two houses there were joined by an arch over a garage. The left-hand house was a miniature of the other. Both red-tiled roofs were fat with snow, which augured well for the heating system. Timber had been combined with gray stone in a pleasant-looking split-level structure that had to be a couple of hundred years old. Curtains were drawn across the windows of the front rooms, blocking any glimpse of the interior. Crying cut the motor. I opened the door.

"You people wait here. I might be some time."

Fat blackbirds were hopping about on the frozen earth. The village below was a collection of smoke spirals against the vivid blue sky. We couldn't have been more than half a mile from Todtsee but the house was completely isolated. A stone shield bearing quartered arms hung above the massive oak door. I yanked on a chain and heard a bell ring somewhere inside. A fat woman opened the door, young, dressed in black, with the chaste suffering face you see on Irish banknotes. Her Swiss-German accent was almost incomprehensible. I could make out no more than "Anna," which seemed to be her name, and "His Highness." She bent down and whisked the powdered snow from my pants with a brush. I followed her into an enormous room where lights were burning dimly. Fawn velvet curtains matched the upholstery of the chairs and sofa. Family portraits and faded photographs decorated the walls. The Aubusson carpet had been mended in several places.

The woman led me to the top of a flight of stone stairs and pointed down silently, as if ushering me into church. We were standing in a gallery, looking down into a dining room where a fire burned in a granite chimney place. The dark furniture was ruddy in the spluttering flames. I could see no use for the bell rope hanging from the beams overhead, except maybe to swing from one side of the gallery to the other. The curtains in the room below were drawn as tight as the others. My eyes gradually adjusted and I made out a figure sitting at the long table. He rose as I made my way downstairs, wiping his mouth on his napkin. He was a couple of inches over six feet with a completely bald head and a face devoid of wrinkles. His skin had the stretched look that is left after plastic surgery. He was wearing a quilted robe over yellow pajama pants, and could have been any age between fifty and seventy. His accent was upper-class English.

"Mr. Paul Henderson? I am Prince Skomielna. Do forgive me for starting without you, but I was so hungry."

A heavy gold bracelet slid up his arm as he gave me his hand. There was a brief yielding of limp fingers. He retrieved them quickly, as if he feared that I was going to break them off and stuff them in my pocket. I dropped into the chair that he indicated.

He lifted the lids on some silver platters. "Tea or coffee?" I helped myself to a plate of kedgeree. I could see him better now. He had green eyes set in a wedge-shaped Tatar face. He drank orange juice from a cut-glass tumbler, displaying a heavy carnelian signet ring on the little finger of his left hand. The movement wafted a smell of Chypre through the aroma of coffee.

"An English breakfast, I'm afraid, Mr. Henderson. Old habits die hard, as they say, and in my country we adopted many English institutions."

I was careful to be courteous, realizing that I had to take the Prince seriously.

"What country was that?"

Chalky white rings surrounded the pupils of his eyes. I tried to remember what they denoted. He answered me blandly.

"I was forgetting — as a Canadian you'd hardly be likely to know. I am Hungarian, Mr. Henderson."

The way he said it conjured up some craggy Transylvanian castle. It wouldn't have been difficult to imagine him being serenaded by gypsy minstrels, while beyond the castle walls white stallions galloped across the steppes.

A clattering of pots and pans behind him located the kitchen. The flames in the fireplace reached out hungrily, illuminating the painted panels and the gallery rails above. Skomielna waved a hand freckled with liver spots.

"Does my house appeal to you?"

I nodded. "What I've seen of it certainly does. It must have been quite a problem getting all this stuff out of Hungary."

I pointed at a suit of armor that stood ghostlike in the corner, the icons on the wall.

"That one is Greek," he said about one of the icons. "Seventeenth-century silver and enamel. It is known as 'Joy to all who suffer' and finds an appropriate home here. In point of fact there are comparatively few things that came here with me from Hungary, Mr. Henderson. That icon happens to be one of them. Perhaps you'd like to hear the story of my exodus. Or not?"

He looked at me slyly and I knew what was expected. "Of course," I said.

He threaded his napkin through a ring with the air of a man who has told the same tale many times but has never tired of it.

"Luck had it that I happened to be on one of my country estates when the Russians invaded Hungary. I woke up one morning to find that my servants had fled during the night taking everything they could lay their hands on. I left with my valet, two dogs, and two polo ponies, traveling in a horse box. All I managed to salvage otherwise was a few family portraits, some *objets d'art*, and my mother's jewelry. She was dead, naturally. An hour or so later, the Communists burned the place down, inspired by my bailiff."

He fitted a cigarette into an amber holder and appeared to be listening to something. After a while I detected the sound of a violin being played somewhere in the house. Skomielna opened his eyes and bawled in German. The violin playing stopped abruptly. He smiled.

"I'm an interior decorator by force of circumstances, Mr. Henderson. I'm lucky enough to know and love beautiful things. This house is an impostor. I built it seven years ago."

A door opened at the far end of the room before I could reply. A boy around eighteen emerged, carrying a violin case. He was dressed in dirty jeans and a sweater, and had a plump face under corn-colored hair. He went by us quickly, flashing the Prince a shy smile. Skomielna waited until he heard the door close upstairs.

"I am a homosexual, Mr. Henderson. I hope the statement doesn't offend you?"

The way he said it, the strange mixture of arrogance and apology knocked me out of stride completely. It was difficult to know how to answer. The easiest way was to speak the truth.

"I'm not that easily offended."

His smile came and went absently. "I'd better start with the fiddle player. It's a little anecdote that illustrates the lengths to which a lonely man will go. The fiddle player is a girl and not a boy. You will appreciate the irony, I'm sure.

I happened to be in a bar in Berne the other night — a homosexual bar, of course. I saw this apparent boy and asked him to dance. He accepted and we fox-trotted together. You're tall like me. You must have noticed that it has the occasional disadvantage. People tend to notice one. A drunk wandered into the bar and seemingly didn't like what he saw. He lurched onto the dance floor and denounced me as a filthy pervert. He even threatened to call the police. Ironical again since the officer in charge of the vice squad is one of us. Put yourself in my place if you can, Mr. Henderson. I travel on a passport issued by the Royal Hungarian Government. I was a career diplomat during the time of the Regency. Now there are only two countries left that recognize a Horthy passport, Spain and Eire. As far as the Swiss are concerned, I am a stateless person. They don't bother me — they even allow me to work here — but I *am* in the country under sufferance. Suddenly I saw myself involved in a monumental scandal. I suppose it was fear that made me clutch the boy tighter. Imagine my amazement, Mr. Henderson, when beneath that shapeless sweater I felt a pair of breasts. Hard, well-developed breasts. I was dancing with a girl. Something that hadn't happened to me in years."

The revulsion on his face made me burst out laughing. "And then?"

He waved his cigarette holder in the air. "Exactly. And then. I speak five languages and a number of dialects — one of them is Swiss-German. I don't know if you've ever been to Berne, but they grunt there like pigs. It is a vernacular that lends itself to coarse abuse. I put this drunk in his place and had him ejected from the bar. I brought the girl back here out of sheer relief. She's a student of music at the *conservatoire* with an unhappy home life. Her genes are obviously confused. She leaves on this evening's train, Mr. Henderson. I never could stand the violin in any case."

He made it all sound so natural that neither of us was embarrassed. He led the way into a studio with skylights cut in the roof. A painter's smock was draped on a chair. There were some good charcoal sketches on the two easels.

"Drawings for Marika's costumes," he said casually. "I'm doing all the *décor* for the ball." He spoke as if he was certain I'd know whom he meant. "There's something I don't quite understand," he added, frowning. "How did this mix-up happen — I mean about your rooms. It's extraordinary. I know Marika's secretary well. Uschi is usually so efficient. This kind of thing is completely out of character."

It dawned on me that he was assuming me to be a guest who had somehow been neglected. I moved my head from side to side.

"I'm not in Todtsee for Miss Bergen's gala. This is probably going to sound like heresy to you, but I've barely heard of her."

He put his hand in the region of his heart, smiling broadly. "That's very good indeed, Mr. Henderson. 'Heresy' is a nice choice of word. It conveys the situation in capsule. Now let me show you the rest of the house."

A back staircase led up to the master suite. The walls were painted pale yellow. A gilt rococo mirror offered a sideways-on view of the swan-shaped bed. There were antique silk carpets on the floor and a bronze-and-ormolu clock ticking away on the mantel. The bathroom was an extension of the bedroom — like the bridge of an ocean liner. There were no dividing walls, nothing more than a couple of steps down.

The elegant tub had spindly silver taps and was set so that the bather's head was level with the window. The view was magnificent, a panorama of frozen peaks ringing the valley. Skomielna opened a door to a dressing room. The first thing I saw was a collection of shoulder-length wigs: blond, red, and black. There was another icon on the wall, otherwise nothing. Skomielna stood at the window, looking down into the garden. The Rolls glittered in the sunshine. Crying Eddie was walking Sophie down the path. Her face peeped out of her hood, her expression adoring.

"Charming," said Skomielna.

I nodded. "My daughter."

Skomielna smiled, but he wasn't putting his heart into it. "I was thinking of your chauffeur. You have no idea what a joy it will be to have properly trained servants in the house again. Mine is a treasure but she's really no more than a peasant."

The corridor ran along the length of the house. He opened one door after another, on bedrooms and bathrooms and finally a small room bright with sunshine. Old hunting prints livened the Regency wallpaper.

"The breakfast room," he said fondly. "English again, you see. It reminds me of my rooms at university. It's possible that this isn't the sort of thing you've been used to, Mr. Henderson. I've never been to Canada. Your customs are probably quite different. If you *do* like the house, I'm afraid I'll have to ask eight thousand francs for a month's let. That would include the maid's wages, the lighting and heating bills, but not the telephone. I expect you'd want to keep in touch with your business interests. I take it you *are* in business?"

It was the first direct question that counted and I treated it accordingly.

"On and off. We've just come from London, where I have friends. But it's difficult with a motherless daughter. Our stay here is a sort of breathing space. I need to think seriously about Sophie's future, and this seemed a good place to do it."

His smile offered a glimpse of capped bicuspids. Everything about him was expensively maintained.

"I'm going to say something that may sound odd, Mr. Henderson. I feel a sort of *rapport* between us. I suppose that's why I talked as indiscreetly as I did just now. I'd like to help make your stay amusing and I have the glimmering of an idea. Let's go down to the drawing room."

The maid had fired the logs in the chimney place. Skomielna sat down on the velvet chaise longue.

"What do you think — about the house, I mean?"

The mirror told me that I wasn't doing badly with the look of faint embarrassment.

"I'm crazy about it, frankly. But what happens to you if we move in?"

He waved the objection out of existence. "I simply transfer to the guesthouse. There's everything I want there, I assure you. And I don't have to go next door to play my piano. You can move your things in right away."

I counted out the money in a sort of dream. He plucked the bills from my fingers, folded them, and stuffed them in a pocket. Then he opened a drawer in a bureau and handed me a colored photograph. It was of Bergen and obviously taken recently. She was posed at the top of some steps in front of a massive door, her figure completely hidden in a sable coat. She was smiling down into the camera.

Skomielna's tone was acid. "One would imagine that she built the place. It's Hari Srinagar's house, of course — Shahpur. The only setting possible for the Snow Queen, naturally. Don't you adore the vulgar rich, Mr. Henderson?"

There was a blond woman standing behind Bergen. "I don't know any," I said, and gave him back the photograph. "Who's the blonde?"

"That's Uschi — Marika's secretary." He had a trick of laughing silently. "One doesn't have to *know* the vulgar rich, Mr. Henderson. One merely observes them. That was the idea I spoke about. Since you are in Todtsee anyway, you should at least see these people making fools of themselves. It's not just the vulgar rich — it's the whole circus, including me. We don't in the least bit mind a critical audience as long as there *is* an audience."

I didn't display too much enthusiasm though adrenalin was making a riptide through my veins.

"I could think of other ways of passing the time," I smiled.

He warmed to his work, leaning forward and tapping me on the knee. "I said there was a *rapport;* let it be Paul and Mischka. You're a man of obvious sensitivity, Paul — I can see that. You spoke of looking for something amusing. All you have to do is give me a hint. I know *everyone.*" He transferred his forefinger to the side of his nose.

"There's one thing you're forgetting," I suggested. "I don't know Miss Bergen nor am I likely to be invited to this ball."

He bared his teeth like an ancient alligator. "Ah, but you will be, dear boy. I can assure you that you will be. Uschi — Baroness Regensdorf — and I have a love-hate relationship that is based on mutual need. And we know too much about one another to be enemies. Leave everything to me. She'll arrange for your invitation. I'll ask her over for dinner to meet you."

He picked up the phone and crooned into the mouthpiece. After a brief conversation in German he put the phone down again.

"I was lucky to catch her in. I don't know what she's up to, but she's behaving rather strangely this last week. One can't apply the word *furtive* to Uschi, but I sense something of the kind. Anyway, the busty baroness honors us with her presence here at eight o'clock. I'll come over a little earlier in case you don't know where everything is. Now let's get your things in!"

The Henderson entourage made a good entrance. Sophie dropped a curtsy for the Prince. The other two waited at attention, just inside the door. Chalice was staring into his bowler like an alms collector into his bowl.

I told them to bring in the suitcases. I walked Sophie across the gallery to the head of the flight of stone steps. I pointed out the perils of a careless descent, but her eyes were on the rope suspended from the rafters.

"What's that for, Papa?" she demanded.

Skomielna touched the top of her head gingerly. "It rings a bell that wakes up the whole village, and we never touch it."

"Why not?" asked Sophie.

He smiled painfully and suggested that the maid show Chalice the kitchen.

"That won't be necessary," I said hurriedly. "He'll find out for himself. In any case he only speaks English."

"Then we'll see one another later," he said.

He went through the door leading out to the garage and guesthouse. A couple of minutes later, Crying Eddie came in, his face as red as a turkey comb.

"What happened?" I said.

He shook his head. "Either I'm losing my mind or that old poof just had a go at me."

Chalice grinned maliciously. "You either got it or you don't, that's what I always say, mate."

Crying Eddie's face was belligerent. "I'll break his bleedin' jaw if he tries it again."

He seemed to be holding me responsible for whatever the Prince had pulled out there.

"He's harmless," I said. "And for the moment we need him."

Eddie's chin lifted. "*I* don't need him, mate. I told you what I bleedin' well need, a good cup of tea."

Chalice groaned. "There he goes with the tea again! We wondered what had happened to you, mate. What took you so long?"

I couldn't help a certain note of complacency creeping into my answer. "We were talking. Bergen's secretary is coming here to dinner tonight. It looks as if I might even get an invitation to the ball."

"You're joking!" said Chalice. Crying Eddie snapped a match between his teeth and eyed me narrowly. Sophie had gone into the kitchen.

"I'm not joking," I said. "She's coming here at eight o'clock and you're serving dinner."

Chalice's face sobered. "Me? You're out of your mind, mate. I can't serve no dinner."

Eddie was leaning against the wall, his eyes half-closed.

"You'll find it comes naturally once you've got that apron on."

"You won't have to cook," I said hurriedly. "I'm going out to the airfield in a minute to see the pilot. I'll stop off at the hotel and order dinner sent up. I'll tell the Prince you're no good cooking in strange kitchens."

Crying Eddie shifted the match from one side of his mouth to the other.

"You're supposed to polish his shoes, too, mate. I seen 'em doing it in the movies."

Chalice shook his head like a wounded bear. "What's this bird coming here for in the first place? A spraunsy like Bergen's ball — with ex-kings and all that lot — and you get invited! It don't make sense to my mind."

I imitated Skomielna's gesture with thumb and forefinger.

"Money," I said. "That's why. The Prince is a keen judge of the scene. He detects the snob behind the millionaire."

"What are you talking about?" Crying Eddie asked disdainfully.

"Just that he's going to help me bribe my way into the ball. My feeling is that there'll be a dozen others like me there. Skomielna and the Baroness probably split the take and the suckers go back to Sarsaparilla Falls and talk about it for the rest of their lives."

Chalice was wearing heavy gold cuff links, out of keeping in a manservant. I reminded myself to tell him about them. I had an idea that both Skomielna and our guest would be observant about that sort of thing.

"You think you might get something out of this bird?" asked Chalice.

86

"That's right," I said easily. "She's Bergen's secretary and everything she says will be of help."

Sophie was at the far end of the room, juggling with a piece of china. A crash interrupted the conversation. We all ran toward the sound. Sophie had her head through the gallery rails and was peering down at what had been a Meissen plate.

"It's only Woolworth's," Chalice said cheerfully.

I took a different tack entirely, bending down and bringing my face close to hers. "You know what happens to little girls who don't do as their fathers say?"

She stared back with blue interested eyes. "They get clobbered."

"Then watch it," I warned.

I found the number of the taxi stand and ordered a cab.

The lobby of the Palace Hotel was deserted except for the house dick. This time he didn't even give me a second glance. One of the clerks telephoned the kitchens for me. It was the sort of place where the chef himself wasn't available but sent one of his aides. I ordered a vichysoisse, avocado pears, tournedos with mushrooms, and babas au rhum. Even Sophie would have been able to serve a meal like that properly. The man from the kitchen suggested that 1937 Moet-et-Chandon was a much neglected wine. I took his word for it and asked him to send up three bottles.

Todtsee airfield turned out to be like a hundred other resort fields. There was one long runway along the spine of the valley. The ring of mountains, looking like a giant hound's tooth, offered a perilously narrow gap as an exit. The terminal building was dominated by a control tower. There were a couple of commercial airliners parked out front of the passenger hall, a small plane, black and silver, outside one of the hangars. I recognized it as a Beechcraft from the pictures they'd shown me in London. A few people were sitting with their baggage in the departure lounge. I spoke to the girl at the Swissair desk and she put Baxter's name over the public-address system. He came from the direction of the bar on the half run, buttoning up his tunic. He was about my own age and build, and redheaded. The freckles across his nose had merged into lemon-colored blotches. He touched the peak of his cap. His accent was the near Cockney that is South African.

"Mr. Henderson? You got my note all right?"

We sat down on a bench some distance from the desk. "I'm sorry about the bed situation, but I'm having the same sort of trouble myself. I'm not staying at the Palace incidentally." I gave him the phone number of Skomielna's house.

He was sitting fairly close and the clove he was chewing failed to disguise the aroma of Scotch. He waved a hand expansively.

"I'm not complaining. They've put me in one of the flight-control cubicles. The bed's comfortable and there's a shower." His eye roved till it found the brunette at the Swissair desk.

I drew him back to the business at hand. "There's been a change in plan, Captain Baxter. My associates are held up in Tokyo. There's nothing that I can do here without them, so you'll be on your own for a couple of days. Just the same you'd better call the house every morning, and if you do leave the field, leave word where you're going. O.K.?"

He got to his feet and flapped a lazy salute. "Whatever

you say, Mr. Henderson. I imagine I'll find something to do. They tell me that a whole lot is happening in town and the place to see the action is the Palace bar."

His attitude was a shade too familiar, and I certainly didn't want to be running into Baxter all over town.

"That could be. But I'll tell you something else. Keep drinking Scotch on an empty stomach and you won't see fifty."

The cab dropped me off downtown and I walked around for a while, getting the feel of the place. By the time I returned to the house it was already dark. All three of them were in the kitchen, a well-equipped room with air extractors and a dish-washing machine. Sophie was perched on a barstool, pushing some scrambled eggs around the plate.

I kicked the snow from my shoes. The cold had left the tip of my nose without feeling. I threw my coat and hat on a chair and sat down close to the heater, looking at Sophie.

"Aren't you just about ready for bed?"

"This isn't a school, is it?" she demanded suspiciously.

I picked her up in my arms. "It's Prince Skomielna's house and he's a very nice man. You be polite to him and stay away from the crockery. Come to think of it, be polite to everyone." I carried her into a studio apartment. The bed was made up with linen sheets and the pillow soft.

"No bath tonight," I said. "Just the face and the hands."

I heard her in the bathroom, trying all the faucets. The *bidet* baffled her completely. When she was done I put Bendy in the bed with her and leaned down. She always smells so good.

"Good night, darling, and don't forget your prayers."

I left the door ajar. Chalice and Crying were in the bed-room they had chosen along the corridor. I could see the crack of light and hear them talking in low voices. I opened the front door. The garden was icy cold. Someone in the guesthouse opposite was playing Chopin. It had to be Skomielna. The boy-girl had left. The two houses were connected by an arched courtyard with a garage at the back. The doors were open. Parked next to the Rolls was an old Porsche Carea. The bodywork was daubed with gray primer paint. I peeped through a slit in the guesthouse curtains. The Prince was sitting with his back to me, his fingers wandering over the keyboard of a Bechstein grand. I let myself into the big house again and called the other two downstairs. Crying Eddie had taken off his tunic, Chalice his tie.

"A dress rehearsal," I said. "Watch carefully." I laid the table in the dining room, finding the place mats and engraved silver side plates. A branched candlestick went in the middle of the gleaming mahogany.

I waved a hand. "Sit down, Eddie. You're the Baroness."

He looked at me a little hard then obeyed. I seated myself opposite him, pointing at the third chair.

"That's the Prince, Harry. We'll be upstairs, the three of us, finishing our drinks. There's a little bell that I tinkle. As soon as you hear it, you come up."

Chalice looked like a Mack Sennett waiter, a napkin draped over his left forearm.

"A little bell," he said earnestly.

Whatever happened I had to be patient. "Take that god-damn napkin off your arm and listen. You wait down here listening for the bell but you keep the kitchen door closed. That's so we don't smell the cooking."

"There ain't going to be no cooking," he said in a puzzled way.

"Just let me write the dialogue," I answered. "You hear the bell and I ask if dinner's ready. Don't forget to say sir and madam and walk down the stairs after us, not in front."

"I know my manners," he said stiffly. Crying Eddie's grin was remote.

Chalice learned quickly, stacking and removing plates, changing the glasses. I left him at it. Crying Eddie had long since made his way upstairs. I found him in front of the fire, watching the flames morosely. I flopped into a chair.

"What's on your mind, Eddie?"

He pushed his legs out, studying me through half-closed eyes. "I don't think Harry'd like it if I told you, mate."

I lit a cigarette. "Chalice isn't here."

He opened his eyes a little wider. I saw the blood rising in his face.

"One of these days," he said softly, "maybe not till this is all over but one of these days, me and you's going to be alone. I'll tell you what's on my mind then. All right?"

"Why not now?" I argued. "This bit that's going on between us is crazy, anyway. What is it that you've got against me, Eddie?"

"You talk too much for one thing. And you never ought to have brought Sophie. Is that enough to be going on with?"

"Too much," I answered. "I know myself better than you do. You keep riding me like this and I'm going to blow higher than Mount Everest. Talking's part of my business, and so is Sophie. I need this job the worst way. All I'm asking is that you get off my back and let me do my job. For Sophie's sake, if that makes things any easier for you."

"You must be kidding," he said, shaking his head. " 'For

Sophie's sake!' The only person you worry about is your-self."

There was a long silence that we both grew tired of. I shifted my legs, still trying to break the deadlock between us.

"Bergen's practicing at the ice stadium tomorrow morning. You could take a look at her if you like. It would help."

"What for?" he asked blankly. "She's not going to do it in her jewelry, is she?"

"No," I agreed. "But the odds are that she'll have some of her bodyguard with her. It would help to know what they look like. I don't expect they move much out of the house. This could be our chance."

He smiled thinly. "Then why don't you do it yourself, mate?"

There was no sense in continuing. It was clear that Eddie wasn't exactly crazy about me. What I'd told him was the truth. I can only take so much of that sort of treatment. I could see no way of averting the showdown that seemed certain to come.

"I'll do just that," I said, and came to my feet. "Remember to keep out of the way when the other people arrive."

The lights were out in Sophie's room. She'd gone to sleep on her stomach with the pillow covering her head. I put her the right way up and she stirred, catching hold of my fingers. I disengaged them gently, telling myself that if I could just push this big one over I'd go by the rules for the rest of my life.

I showered and put on a dark blue suit with button-down shirt and sober tie. An image of sober North American respectability stared back at me from the mirror. I was still admiring it, when I sensed rather than heard someone behind me. Skomielna came around the door, an out-stretched arm making apology.

"I'm so sorry, I should have knocked It was pure force of habit. May I come in?"

"You're already in," I said shortly. He hadn't put a foot wrong with me and yet I had a creepy feeling being up here alone with him. He was wearing a cream-colored Nehru tunic with matching pants and a pair of buckled shoes. The chain slung around his neck supported a large amber stone that could well have been a topaz.

His green slanted eyes were missing nothing, taking in the Vuiton traveling bags, the money and passport on the table, the clothes that I had unpacked.

"I forgot my wigs," he said casually, offering no further excuse or explanation. He came out of the dressing room, all six of them dangling from his hand. He put the next question suddenly and with no hint that he was switching languages.

"*Wo schläft das Kind?*"

My reflexes were a fraction of a second too quick for my brain. I had already made an instinctive gesture toward Sophie's bedroom. He smiled, putting me in mind again of an ancient alligator.

"So you do speak German after all. You know, I thought you might. Very well, my dear, I'll leave you to finish dressing."

I sat down on the bed for a while, thinking. The 'my dear' was harmless enough — a literal translation from either French or German. What bothered me was the look in his eye. It was almost conspiratorial. The tale of the Trojan Horse kept coming into my head but I couldn't remember how the end went. It was getting close to half after seven when I went down to the drawing room. The velvet curtains had been drawn. The flames leaped in the stone fireplace. I fixed myself a much needed drink and looked over the gallery rails. Chalice had lit the candles. The silver gleamed in their soft light.

A quarter to eight. The tires of the hotel wagon whispered over the rock-hard snow outside. I went out to the kitchen. A man carried in a trolley that was laden with metal platters. They had provided spirit lamps to keep the food hot, and the bottles of champagne nestled in a bed of cracked ice. The spray of orchids came with the compliments of the management. I paid the bill and shut the kitchen door. Chalice was looking at the trolley doubtfully.

"You're sweating," I said. "For crissakes, try to relax. All you have to do is remember the golden rule — everything from the left-hand side."

He shook his head, lounging closer as I lit the spirit lamps. "It ain't that that's worrying me, mate. It's you and Eddie."

I blew out the match. The orchids were like a piece of painted flesh and completely without smell.

"Why don't you try talking to him about it?" I suggested. "I already have and it got me nowhere."

He'd changed his shirt and removed the massive gold cuff links. The sideburns were right for a gentleman's gentleman, but there was still something about the production that was dead wrong. It was something about the way he moved. It would have been simple to have a waiter in from the hotel to serve the meal. Looking at Chalice, I wondered why I hadn't done it.

"He's got an idea that you're having a go at him all the time," he said. "He's touchy over little things."

My amazement was genuine. "Over *what* little things? I treat him like a *prima donna!*"

He had the grace to look uncomfortable. "I know, mate. It's his glands. It can't be healthy living the way he does. No booze, no smoking, no birds, and all this muscle-building. I'll have another word with him. How do I look?"

"Impeccable," I said. "Just remember the golden rule."

He smiled in a sick sort of way and wheeled the trolley into the dining room. I was working on my second drink when Skomielna came across from the guesthouse. He stopped just inside the door, clasped his hands, and sniffed dramatically.

"*Saude Smitane!* Delicious."

He smiled, his aquiline nostrils still flaring as he poured himself a large-sized jolt of vodka. He drank it neat and without ice. He wiped his mouth, putting his bald head to one side.

"I hear a car. It has to be Uschi. The Germans are always punctual."

He reached the door at precisely the right moment to open it for our guest. He lifted her hand to his lips and helped her off with her cloak. For some reason or other, the gesture reminded me of unpeeling a banana. Baroness Regensdorf was even more striking than in the pictures I'd seen. She was very tall with hair the color of newly planed pine. She wore it low on her neck, a bun skewered by a tortoise-shell spike. Her icy blue eyes were faintly contemptuous behind severe-looking spectacles. An artist had fashioned her tan silk trouser suit to demonstrate a magnificent bust and behind. She looked to me to be in her late twenties.

She and the Prince greeted one another like boxers who are called to the center of the ring and told to touch gloves and come out fighting. Her smile revealed good teeth a little on the small side. Skomielna's introduction was skittish.

"Mr. Paul Henderson, Uschi! Paul — this is Baroness von und zu Regensdorf."

I detected a note of mockery but she showed no sign of having noticed it. I recognized the whiff of Nina Ricci as she gave me her hand. Her English was perfect with British vowel sounds and inflections.

"It's very kind of you indeed to invite me, Mr. Henderson."

This time the smile baffled me. If Skomielna was serious, we were here to arrange a rather questionable deal in which I paid money for admission to her employer's ball. But she was behaving as if it were no more than an enjoyable social occasion between old friends.

"My pleasure," I answered, standing until she took a seat on the sofa.

"So there we are, my dears," the Prince said lightly. "A Balt and a Canadian. That should make for pepper in the air. What will you drink, Uschi, my love?"

She had taken off her spectacles. Her face was much less placid without them. The distance between her cheekbones seemed to me to be wider, her teeth sharper. If people were animals, I thought, this one was a leopard. A snow leopard. Her cobalt eyes assessed me unwinkingly over her glass of *amontillado*. Suddenly she passed the tip of her tongue lightly over her lower lip. It was done deliberately while Skomielna's back was turned. We chatted for a few moments, the decline of the Côte d'Azur, the difficulty of finding a governess for Sophie — that sort of thing. Nobody mentioned Bergen or the ball. When the glasses were empty I rang the small silver bell and Chalice appeared at the top of the stone stairs. He went into a sort of sideways shuffle that he must have been practicing specially. His bloodhound eyes took in the Prince's attire without any change of expression.

"Dinner's served," he said ungraciously. At least he didn't add "mate."

Skomielna made a half-bow in my direction that told me I was meant to give the Baroness my arm. Her fingers rested on it lightly yet firmly. We walked downstairs like a couple in a scene from *Rupert of Hentzau*. The firelight revived itself in the silverware, in the suit of armor. The Baroness removed the spray of orchid from her napkin and tucked it in the V of her shirt. I signaled to Chalice and he eased the cork from the first bottle of champagne. He poured the wine, holding his left hand behind his back. The bottle seemed to be shaking a little but I was the only one to notice it. The other two seemed to have accepted anything bizarre in Chalice's behavior as English eccentricity. I raised my glass to each of my guests in turn.

"Never above you, never beneath you, but always at your side!"

Skomielna drank and then beat his palms together softly. "Bravo. A charming toast. Is it Canadian?"

"Danish, I think," I answered, aware of the Baroness's covert inspection. She was doing it in a way that suggested she didn't want Skomielna to notice. The meal progressed. By all the rules of the game, Chalice should have produced some gaffe that would have blown his cover, but he served unobtrusively though breathing hard. The food was excellent, the steak melted under the knife — the baba was soaked in rum and garnished with unsweetened whipped cream.

We were working on the last bottle of wine. That is, the Prince and I were. Two glasses appeared to be the Baroness's limit.

Skomielna finally got around to sounding out my finances. The moment he started I realized I was in the hands of an expert. He slipped easily from the rigors of Canadian taxation, stayed for a while with mutual funds, and finished in praise of a Swiss domicile. The whole thing took him maybe twenty minutes and at the end of it all he had a detailed picture of the Henderson interests that was completely misleading. Baroness Regensdorf's ears might have been for the Prince, but her eyes were still on me. Her pose, chin in hand, offered a fair view down the front of her silk shirt. That, too, she knew. I was convinced of it. She acknowledged key questions in Skomielna's cross-examination by a touch of the hand to the back of her pale, coiled hair or the lengthening of an eyebrow.

We went upstairs for coffee and brandy. Skomielna sat down, shaking his back coquettishly. It might have been some raven mane that he had instead of a bald bony scalp.

"Let's get down to the point, Uschi. Don't you think, now that you've met him, that Mr. Henderson ought to be invited to Marika's ball?"

I tried to look modest as she turned her ankle and considered the heel of her crocodile shoe.

"I agree," she said graciously. "I think he'd be an asset."

My mumble of protest went unnoticed. Skomielna's stretched face widened to a smile of satisfaction.

"You can handle the Snow Queen?"

She wiped away the faint mustache of coffee that stained her upper lip.

"Marika's no problem. She doesn't know half the people she's invited anyway. Tell me, Mr. Henderson. You're a man of the world, obviously much traveled. What do you find about a middle-aged woman's vanity that interests you?"

This was between her and me. Skomielna's eyes were fixed on the ceiling. I finished the brandy in my glass.

"What interests the rest of her guests?" I parried.

Her hand turned on her wrist elegantly. "That's much easier to answer. Snobbishness and vanity. They need one another's company to prove they're the people society journalists write about. Others couldn't care less as long as they're expensively entertained at someone else's expense. You don't seem to fall into either of these categories."

I lifted a shoulder. "I'm not even sure that I want to go."

She looked at me coolly. "Of course you do, otherwise you wouldn't have engineered this dinner date. Don't treat me as a fool, Mr. Henderson. Please."

I changed tack hastily. "I guess it's a sort of resentment. I can assure you of one thing — when I arrived here this morning, all I knew about Marika Bergen was that they market skates in Canada with her name on them. First thing I know, I can't get accommodation for my daughter and myself because this woman's booked out every hotel for her guests. Then Mischka mentioned the ball. I felt it might be a good way of reinflating my ego."

Skomielna rose, blocking a yawn. His wink told me that I'd said the right thing.

"It's past midnight and I have a busy day tomorrow. You won't mind if I leave you."

He opened the door, shivered theatrically, and ran across

the courtyard. The Baroness fished in her purse for a cigarette and waited for me to light it. She let the smoke dribble
from half-open lips. I'd seen it done better.

"You've promised Mischka money, of course," she said.
"Naturally."

"Give him nothing," she said definitely. "I'll tell you something, Mr. Henderson. You intrigue me and I like being
intrigued."

I was suddenly very uneasy. It had been a long time since
a woman like this had made an open play for me. I threw a
log on the fire and stood up.

"Excuse me for a moment. I have to take a look at my
daughter."

Sophie was fast asleep. I sat down on the other bed, trying to rationalize the Baroness's behavior. The obvious answer was that when something rich and unattached came
into range she let fly with both barrels. She was staring
into the flames when I went back. She started as though I'd
scared her.

"What do you call your daughter?"

"Sophie Matilda," I said, and sat down beside her aware
that I'd had too much to drink.

"They're beautiful names," she said softly. "She must
mean a great deal to you."

"Everything." My voice was too loud and I lowered it.
"She's all I have."

She made a small movement of the head as if she understood. "I hope you'll let me see something of her while you're
here, Paul. Do you mind me calling you Paul?"

My arm was on the back of the sofa, my hand almost
touching her neck. She stayed exactly as she was, neither
moving away from or toward my fingers.

"I'd like to think you'll be seeing something of me too," I suggested.

Her eyes narrowed as she smiled. "That's really what I meant."

This was heady stuff but I took a calculated chance. "How about tomorrow morning for breakfast?"

She laughed and reached for her cape. "I think that's a little premature. I have to work for a living, anyway. I go out very little, really. Tonight was an exception."

I still didn't know why. "You could take time out for a drink, surely," I protested.

I was standing close behind her, holding her cape. She turned her head, her expression suddenly serious.

"I'd like that, Paul. Meet me in the Gambrinus Bar at twelve-thirty tomorrow morning. It's a quiet place on Bahnhofstrasse opposite the post office. Nobody one knows ever goes there. You'd be perfectly safe."

I settled the cloak on her shoulders. " 'Safe' seems an odd word to use."

"I meant safe from gossip," she explained. "To all intents and purposes you're a bachelor and Todtsee is full of beautiful women. I wouldn't want to spoil your chances." Her fingertips touched my cheek for the briefest of seconds.

Outside, a cold moon hung in a frigid sky. A bough in a nearby tree cracked sharply as we walked across to the parked BMW. It was black with a Hamburg registration. She gave me her hand.

"Good night, Paul. I am very glad that I met you."

I watched the taillights of the sedan through the gates and down the slope out of sight. The guesthouse was in darkness. I double-locked the front door and headed for bed. As I went through the drawing room, I noticed Uschi's spectacle case. I picked it up, meaning to return it the following morning. I don't know what made me open the suede holder but I did. The lenses of her spectacles were made of plain glass.

Chalice and Crying were sitting up in bed, waiting to hear my report. I peered in at them, a hand on each side of the doorway. Crying Eddie lowered the corners of his mouth, registering disapproval.

"He's stoned, Harry. Stoned out of his bleedin' mind."

I wagged my head, grinning at him. "No more than pleasantly loaded. The Baroness is providing me with an invitation to Bergen's ball. I'm meeting her tomorrow morning. Like Harry said, some have it and some don't."

He was reading a copy of *The Weightlifter*, a magazine devoted to the manipulation of loaded bars. He threw it on the floor with a gesture of disgust.

"You'd better sober up before tomorrow morning. You can't even stand straight, look at you!"

"Belt up and go to sleep if you can't be civil," Chalice admonished. "That's great, Paul, really great news."

Crying wasn't finished. "Nobody ain't told me why a bird like this baroness does her nut the moment she meets him! A baroness and mixing with the cream. It don't make bleedin' sense!"

"I agree," I said with dignity. My head was beginning to spin. "You need to have imagination for the maneuver to make sense. Good night."

Sleep came as a long drop through ever-dimming lights with Crying Eddie's voice echoing down the tunnel after me.

Chapter Four

MORNING WAS CLEAR, hard and bright through the bedroom windows. I ungummed my eyes and stumbled down to the bath. Hot water and a couple of aspirins eased the ache from my body and brain. I could hear steel runners screaming as a bobsled sliced down the run beyond the garden walls.

I found Chalice in the kitchen, leaning against the dishwashing machine, his face morose in repose. He was watching Sophie and Crying bombarding one another with snowballs out in the garden. I lowered myself gingerly onto one of the tall stools. The coffee was still hot. I poured myself a bowlful from the pot. I drank it, shuddered, and lit a cigarette.

"Did the maid show?"

Chalice stopped the clatter of the machine. "She's upstairs making the beds. She's been getting on my nerves. She creeps around putting her finger on her lips and saying, 'Ssshhh.'"

"It's the Prince," I explained. "He likes to sleep on in the mornings."

He shook his head. "Wait till Doll hears about all this. Princes, baronesses. She'll do her nut, thinking that she missed it. That Baxter phoned from the airfield wanting to know whether you'd got any instructions for him. I said no. All right?"

I was wearing a pair of corduroy pants, a turtleneck sweater, and my suede jacket. I wound my watch and set it by the kitchen clock, twenty minutes to eleven. I peered out of the window again. Sophie and her friend had vanished in the tangle of spruce on the south side of the garden.

"Try to keep her amused," I said. "I don't know how long it'll be before I'm back. I thought I might take a look at the stadium before I meet the Baroness. Get a close-up of Bergen's bodyguard."

His dark eyes lingered on my shaking fingers. "You're the boss, mate. You're the one who's making the decisions. All I ask you to do is make the right ones. You know my meaning, Paul. This coup has *got* to be right."

There was an undertone in his voice that reminded me who and what he really was — a professional thief who had parlayed his courage and intelligence into a fortune. But there was more to it than that. It told me that, more than anything else before, success mattered now. Chalice wanted a place in the halls of criminal fame.

He removed his back from the dish-washing machine, transformed by the smile on his face.

"It's *got* to be right," he said again with even more emphasis.

"It will be," I said quietly. "I can't afford to blow this any more than you can."

I promised to have some groceries sent up from the village and started on my walk downtown. Overloaded busses were crawling up to the ski lifts and mountain restaurants. The sunshine was dazzling, the sidewalks bright with vinyl anoraks and matching pants. Faces wearing enormous round glasses peered out from under shaggy goatskin hats. The ice stadium had the same deserted look as the previous day. The sound of recorded music echoed inside. I walked around to the back.

A Cadillac limousine was parked in front of one of the side entrances. The chauffeur at the wheel lowered his newspaper as I went by. I had a glimpse of a mink lap robe bundled up on the back seat. The path I had taken circled the rear of the stadium, at the same time serving as a short cut to the frozen lake. One more bend put me out of sight of the chauffeur. I lit a cigarette, wasting time in case he'd left the car and followed me. I could see a couple of jockeys down below, cantering their mounts around the snowbound circuit. The high blowing of the horses, the six-eight timing of their thudding hooves, carried clearly in the thin still air. I could see no one any nearer than that.

Covered ways led to numbered entrances into the stadium. I ran down the first passage on my left. The doors at the end were held firmly on the inside by push bars. All I'd brought with me was a strip of mica, expecting to have to deal with a simple spring lock. It was useless on a door of this kind. I went outside again. Plows had been used to clear the parking lot and pathways. The snow had been left in hard ridged banks driven tight up against the walls. There was no one to see me clamber up and put my heel against a window. I pulled the broken glass out and stuck my arm through. I could just reach the catch and release it. I scrambled through the window and dropped down to a drafty passage running underneath the spectator benches.

There were steps to the stadium proper only a few yards away. I inched up, head low and holding my hat in my hands. I came out cautiously, finding myself in back of what would have been the north goal in a hockey match.

The music stopped abruptly, leaving a woman's voice echoing through the stadium, shrill and complaining. Marika Bergen was on the ice. A small group of people were standing on the other side of the boards. She was wearing a short-sleeved and short-skirted black dress with pleats and black leather trimmings. Two strings of beads dangled around her neck and she wore elbow-length gloves. Her blond hair cascaded down under a red fox hat as far as her shoulders. Her legs looked twenty years younger than the rest of her body.

She had the sort of face that is pretty when young, piggish forever afterward. There was something about the tilted nose over an angry mouth that was particularly unattractive.

"I must have music to skate to," she bawled in English. "I cannot skate to *click-click-click!*"

The sound engineer fiddled with the controls on his console. The music started again. The two men standing behind the engineer were unmistakably cops. There's something about the law that one learns to recognize at sight. An air of posed purpose — a trick of being able to look in all directions at the same time. More than anything, it's the complete lack of humor in their faces. If a cop smiles it's usually because somebody's broken a leg. They were both wearing Lake Michigan gear, woolen caps with earflaps and heavy mackinaws. Each was in his fifties and chewing gum in a dedicated sort of way. My guess was that they were a couple of retired legmen picking up easy money with the Slade Agency.

The music swelled into Berlioz's *Les Francs-Juges* and Bergen glided away on one leg, holding her body horizontal to the ice. She went into a spin as the music quickened, one knee raised, her arms crossed on her chest. She was moving so fast at the end that her body became a blur. Her skates struck sparks as she braked to an abrupt finish. The sound engineer and the two cops started to clap their hands. She skated over to the boards, peeling off her gloves.

"What the hell are you clapping for, you idiots! I was terrible. Turn that noise off — I've had enough for today."

I used a convenient exit, leaving the bar up and the door open. According to what I'd read, Bergen had already given five farewell performances. It seemed significant to me that none of her friends had been present at the stadium, not even the Baroness. By the time I had walked around to the front of the stadium, the Cadillac had gone. I bought an armful of magazines at a newsstand on Bahnhofstrasse. One of them had a feature on the Bergen jewelry. I put it away for future reading.

The sun seekers were stretched out on chairs on the Palace Hotel terrace, greasy faced, their glued eyes turned heavenward. There was an Italian grocery store nearby, where the manager promised to deliver food within the hour. It was almost noon when I located the Gambrinus, obliquely across from the post office.

It was a badly lit cellar bar with a tiny glass dance floor and bandstand. The barman doubled as waiter. He carried a beer to a table I'd taken at the bottom of the stairs. There was a mirror opposite that gave me a clear view of the entrance upstairs. I opened the copy of *Paris-Match* and started reading about Marika Bergen's jewelry. The article was illustrated by a double spread of color photographs. I was halfway through it when I heard footsteps at the top of the stairs. A pair of shoes came into view, then the legs, and then a bulky gray overcoat. The threat of impending disaster came up as clear as a road sign ahead.

A fat red-faced man stopped at the foot of the stairs, shaking his smooth silver head at me benevolently. "For a moment there I thought you were hiding from me. Don't mind if I sit down for a moment, do you?"

His accent was undiluted Australian. He whipped a chair under his butt without waiting for my answer. Greasy George Gorbals' victims have exhausted the English language trying to describe him. No one has done it to complete satisfaction. Gorbals is a combination of police informer and extortioner with a talent for being in the right place at the appropriate moment. He smells impending larceny as a buzzard does death, and operates with the same lack of charity. People have broken both his kneecaps so that he moves at a sort of jog. He's been shot at three times and twice left for dead. He's bad news, completely fearless, and hot to handle. Killing him has always seemed the only way of dealing with the bastard, and here he was sitting down at my table. Any moment now and the Baroness would be arriving. I started to get to my feet but he waved me back, his snake's eyes snapping.

"Where you going, mate? All I want is a little chat."

He unbuttoned his coat and let his breath out, looking at me as if I was the Prodigal Son to be prayed over and nourished. The barman brought him a glass of Vichy water. Gorbals sipped at it judiciously.

"They told me you'd turned it in a year ago. They said you'd lost your nerve and gone peddling encyclopedias on the American bases. That doesn't sound like Henderson to me, I said. He's got too much class for that, I said. Far too much class!"

My exposures to Greasy George had been infrequent enough. I used to see him in the winter whenever I went to the track. He was around Chelsea for a while with a red-headed girl he claimed was his niece and who committed suicide. But I'd never had him on my tail, never had a drink with him, never even spoken to him except in the company of others.

"I'm busy," I said shortly. "Make it some other time."

He grinned as though I'd just paid him a compliment, reached out, and took the copy of *Paris-Match*. He opened it at the article on Bergen. His tone was conversational.

"I heard the BBC news this morning. There's no racing in England today. All the jumping meetings are frozen off. Still and all, there are better ways of making money — right, Paul, boy?"

I kept my mouth shut. He went on reminiscently. "The long arm of coincidence, isn't that what they call it? I was in Sammy Kline's steam bath last Friday trying to get rid of some of this fat and who comes in but that Crying Eddie. He gives himself a workout in the gym, dives into the cold pool, and comes and lies down a few cubicles away from me. Didn't notice me, of course. He was too busy reading his book."

"What is it you want from me?" I snarled.

He held up a pudgy hand. "Don't be in such a hurry, mate. That's half the trouble today; people are always in a hurry. This fellow came on television the other night and said the art of conversation's been lost. He's dead right."

"Nobody with all his marbles would want to practice the art of conversation with you, you creep. Are you going to get out of here and let me alone, or do I throw you out?"

"*Throw* me out?" he said in a pained fashion. "I'm talking about your new friend, Crying Eddie! Strange enough to catch him reading a book, but when I saw the title I almost flipped. *Switzerland: Europe's Winter Wonderland.*" He smiled at me like some benevolent uncle sharing a joke with a favorite nephew.

I pushed my chair back quickly, knowing what was coming. And before it came I had to head off the Baroness. Greasy George's face drew together. His mouth was pursed and mean.

"Don't run, mate. That'd be the very worst thing you could do."

I dropped back in my seat. False bonhomie flooded into his face again, and he started reading from the article on Bergen's jewelry.

"'A pair of diamond ear pendants. Each earring is composed of a large emerald-cut diamond, diamond held by a similarly cut stone and with a drop-diamond cloverleaf. The pendants were once the property of Pauline Borghese.'" He looked up over his spectacles. "Never knew I could speak French, did you, mate? Two years in Fresnes Prison and me but a lad. Now listen to this! 'An emerald-cut pink diamond necklace, a cushion-shaped diamond weighing one hundred and five carats, a diamond stomacher once given by ex-King Farouk to an English actress.' And all that gear owned by one woman. It's an invitation to crime, that's what it is. It'd serve her right if somebody robbed her." He took off his spectacles and pushed the magazine across the table, shaking his head like a preacher scenting sin in the congregation.

The bar was still empty. I had exactly eleven minutes left before the Baroness showed up. I kept my voice low, but I was unable to control its angry shake.

"I'm wise to your goddamn tricks, Gorbals. But this time it won't work."

He wiped his mouth. "I haven't finished yet, Paul. You'd better hear the end of it before you start making remarks like that. This place ain't big enough for you mugs to wander about and not be seen. I've been sitting around the Palace Hotel for three days now waiting for a familiar face to show up. I almost fell off my chair when I saw the three of you come into the lobby. Eddie in those breeches and Chalice in a bowler!"

I leaned forward so that the barman couldn't hear. "I said it won't work. They'll kill you, George, and I'm not bluffing."

I might have just told him the one about the bishop and the chorus girl he laughed so heartily.

"*Kill* me, mate! Don't you understand that I'm on your side! If I wasn't, you would never have got out of that hotel yesterday. There were three local law in the lobby not counting the house cop. They've run nine thieves out of town in the last week, French and Italian mobs. What they're doing is meeting the planes and the trains and just turning the villains around. You three are the only starters from the home mob. That's how much I'm on your side. I want to talk to Chalice."

The hands of the clock had crept on another five minutes.

"The first thing he'll ask is what you want," I answered. "You'd better tell me. And tell me where he can meet you."

He smiled. Anyone looking at him would have seen a

kindly old gaffer passing on a word of advice to a younger friend.

"I'll come by the house about six. I know where you're living. Tell Chalice I want twenty grand, payable in advance."

It was the bit about knowing where we lived that crippled the last of my restraint. I saw my face in the mirror, savage with anger.

"I hope he does kill you. I'm going to get a lot of pleasure out of helping to bury you!"

The waiter had moved nearer and was polishing a corner table. Greasy George chuckled away as if I'd said something amusing.

"I like a bloke with spirit. That little girl looks as if she's inherited some of it from you. Don't forget then, tell Chalice six o'clock. Don't worry about a thing — I won't embarrass you." He lifted his hat in farewell and climbed up to the street. It was only after he'd gone that I realized he'd left me to pay for his Vichy water.

Baroness Regensdorf was punctual to the minute. She hurried down the stairs, unfastening the belt of a bleached sealskin coat. She looked around, found me, and waved. She took off the matching pillbox hat, letting the mass of pale hair fall around her shoulders. When I greeted her, she left her fingers in mine, ordering a glass of lemon juice without bothering to turn her head toward the waiter.

"Something's upset you," she challenged immediately. "I can tell. Your eyes grow darker when you're angry."

I pushed the spectacles case across the table. "You forgot this last night."

She dropped the case in a patent-leather purse, still hanging on to my hand.

"You're not angry with me, are you?" I shook my head. "Say 'No, Uschi. I'm not angry with you.' Come on, say it!"

No woman looks at a man the way she was looking at me unless she means business, but I was thinking of something else. I was thinking of my partners' reaction when I broke the news that Greasy George was in town. Illogically enough, I felt guilty about it — as if it were something that I should have been able to forestall.

"Consider it said," I answered. "I had a phone call that I could have done without. It's nothing more than that."

"A phone call from a woman?" She snapped her lighter, holding her hair away from the flame as she lit her cigarette.

"Nothing as romantic, I'm afraid. A business matter. Look, let me ask *you* a question, Uschi. What's the reason for wearing fake spectacles?"

She laughed, throwing her head back, showing her magnificent throat.

"I see. You're not only rich and handsome, you're observant as well. That's a dangerous combination for a woman to have to deal with. I'll tell you. The spectacles are meant to detract from any other interest I might have. My employer insists on it. She says spectacles give me an air of responsibility. She likes the idea."

"She's really as bad as that?" I asked curiously.

"Worse," she said. "Far, far worse. Would you like to know what I'm thinking at this very moment?"

In some incredible way her fingers were still locked in mine. "It couldn't do any harm," I answered lightly.

She pulled my arm around so that we both faced the mirror. Her reflection smiled back at me.

"I was thinking that we make a handsome couple. There are things that I could teach you, you know, Paul."

It was the fastest proposition that had come my way in a long time and by far the most unlikely. I moved my shoulders briefly, freeing my fingers in the process.

"I've no doubt about it. What puzzles me is why you'd bother."

She leaned her chin in her hand, studying my face. "And what puzzles me is your modesty. I thought all men were conceited."

"They're conceited all right," I allowed. "But some of us are wary. It all has to do with making a fool of yourself. Do you understand what I'm trying to say?"

She turned the corners of her mouth down. "Only partly, I'm afraid. Couldn't you put it into plainer words, Paul?"

I lit a cigarette of my own, brushed the smoke away from between us, and did just that.

"I gave you a reason last night, why I wanted to get into this ball of Bergen's. I said it was pique. Well, that's only half the reason. I was trying to analyze it just now, walking down from the house. There's curiosity in there somewhere as well, Uschi. I want to see these people in the flesh — these people who make the gossip columns year in, year out. O.K., that's my side of it. Let's get to yours. You're in a position where you can get me an invitation to this junket. Skomielna suggested you'd do it for money. You say you don't want money, which leaves me wondering exactly why you're giving me a come-on like a Montreal B-girl."

I watched the pulse beating beneath the skin of her finely molded throat. I shifted my gaze to her eyes as she laughed. She sounded genuinely amused.

"My poor Paul, what sort of women have you known, for goodness sake! Do you think there's some sort of *mystique* about being a baroness? There were seven at my last school. Most of them were poor, dowdy, and stupid. One was a nymphomaniac at sixteen. I've never been to Montreal, and I don't know too much about the way a B-girl operates. But if someone like you arrives on the scene, someone who could offer the means of escape, I imagine she'd use all her wiles and wit to hook him. In that sense, you're right, I suppose. I'm acting like a B-girl."

"But you're not working in a clip joint, Uschi," I argued. "What dreadful fate am I supposed to be offering escape from?"

"One of these days I'll tell you," she promised. "I've watched you move and smile, listened to the way you talk about your daughter. I don't know about love, but I know about having a fancy for someone. I'm sure I could teach you how to relax, Paul. I want you to take me with you when you leave. Who knows how long it will last — we'll have as much chance as anyone else. And if it does come to an end, we'll be able to say good-bye graciously. Isn't that some sort of basis for an honest bargain?"

I looked at her sharply. She was dead serious. "You haven't even asked whether I'm divorced or involved with somebody else."

"That's right," she said steadily. "The offer still stands."

"And Marika?"

She snapped her thumb and forefinger. "I can leave at any time. All we have is a verbal agreement. She wouldn't hesitate to break it when it suits her."

I was finding the dialogue difficult to control. "Look," I

said. "I've got to get back to the house now. I've got to take a call from Winnipeg. Isn't there some way we could continue this conversation later?"

She nodded, reaching for her pillbox hat. "I can come to your house at quarter after three. I know the maid leaves at three. Would you like me to do that, Paul?"

The brakes were off and this thing was running away with me. "You're forgetting a few people. Skomielna, my daughter, the servants."

She spoke carelessly, as if assignations were simple to arrange. "There's a children's playground behind the Post Hotel. Send your daughter there with the servants. Mischka will be at Shahpur until six."

She rose, blew me a kiss, and vanished.

I waited for five minutes before following her upstairs. I crossed the street, went into the post office, and called a Geneva number. Scotty Dundas had been in that city for three years, linkman for a bunch of Italian forgers operating out of Milan. My credit rating might have been low in orthodox circles, but on the other side of the fence it was limitless. I asked Scotty what he had on offer, made a bid, and was promised delivery by mail the next day.

I got back to the house to find Crying Eddie and Sophie still horsing around in the garden. I called him over. We went inside and located Chalice in the cellar. He'd locked himself in there with his book on Rommel. He opened the door suspiciously. I pushed by, turned, and addressed them both.

"Brace yourselves for a shock. Greasy George Gorbals is in town. I just left him. He says he wants twenty grand or he'll blow the whistle on us. He's coming up here tonight."

The cellar had the same deceptive appearance of age as the rest of the house. Part of it was evidently used as a lumber room. Cobwebs festooned the wine bins and barrels. Crying's face was incredulous in the light from the naked bulb hanging from the ceiling.

"Coming up here!"

I moved a shoulder. Chalice put his book down very carefully. "They try to cure cancer. You can go in a bleedin' flophouse these days and not find a bedbug, but nobody does anything about Greasy George."

"*I'll* do something about him," Crying Eddie said menacingly. His tone of voice made my toes curl.

"I know how to handle him," I broke in hurriedly.

"So do I, mate," Eddie rejoined, swinging around at me. "Put a hole in the back of his head."

Chalice's swarthy features were expressionless. I lifted myself from the edge of the barrel.

"Five minutes to pack — that's all I need — and I'll leave you guys to it. 'A hole in the back of his head'! Where do you think you are?"

Crying seemed to drift somewhat in my direction, chin cocked. "How come Greasy George is here in the first place?"

"A good question," I said. "As a matter of fact, he told me. He spotted you in Sammy Kline's last Friday reading a book about Switzerland. It seems this gave him an idea. The rest is easy to understand. He knew about the Bergen hoopla. He makes it his business to know this kind of thing. So he turned up here and waited for us to arrive. He even knew where we're living."

Crying Eddie rapped his forehead with the heel of his hand. "What can you do with a bastard like that!"

"The thing is that he's here," Chalice said quietly. "The geezer's a bleedin' menace. Look what he done to the twins when they wouldn't pay off. Set them up for that insurance thing and then give evidence against them. I heard it. I was sitting in court. The judge called him Mr. Gorbals and carried on about his courage to stand up fearlessly and tell the truth about a wicked conspiracy. They even give Greasy thirty quid expense money. One thing's for sure — he always means what he says."

Eddie's words added a chilling postscript. "I'll do him myself, Harry. You two don't have to know nothing about it."

I could hear Sophie's laughter somewhere in the house, and here was Eddie talking about killing a man in cold blood. I lit a cigarette, trying to control my fingers as I did so.

"Then you can count me out. I just can't be a party to it."

Crying Eddie's face was sculptured in granite. "*Now* do you see what I mean, Harry! He's a false-pretenser, the geezer. All he wants to do is play the clown at our expense."

"Come off it," Chalice said quickly. "Don't be that way, Ed."

"What other way is there to be?" retorted his partner. "We're sticking our necks out with him. I got the right to know how we stand."

The atmosphere was tense. I dropped the butt on the brick floor and ground my heel on it.

"I never ran out on a deal in my life," I said stubbornly. "But I was never involved in murder either."

"Forget it," said Chalice. "What me and Eddie's trying to do is find a way to deal with Greasy George. If you don't like his way, why don't you tell us yours?"

I shook my head impatiently. "Because you haven't asked me. When Greasy comes up here tonight, he'll expect to be insulted. Threaten him if you like. Then when he finally shows his hand, tell him it'll take time to produce that kind of money. Say you can get it by tomorrow. He's no fool. He doesn't think you'll be carrying twenty grand around with you."

Crying Eddie spoke with the barest movements of his lips. "He won't go for that any more than I would, mate."

I ignored him, concentrating on Chalice. "Greasy's eyes and ears are everywhere. He's already made up his mind that it's Bergen's gear we're after. He can't know about the gas or that we're going to take the whole goddamn assembly."

Chalice frowned. "Let's look at it this way. What's the worst he can do to us?"

I considered the question before I answered. "At the moment, no more than have us run out of town as undesirables. You two get rid of your passports and we haven't broken any laws. But that finishes us, of course. He'll have studied all the implications, gone through the possibilities. My guess is that he's satisfied nobody will make a hit till Bergen's jewelry comes out of the safe on the night of the ball. If he thinks he'll get his money before then, he'll go for the tale."

Chalice's hand was covering his nose, his dark brown eyes half closed.

"You mean we're going to pay this bastard twenty thousand quid?"

I told him the facts. "In hundred-dollar bills. George isn't going to know this, but they're phony. The guy holding them is a pal of mine. I called him from the village and bought twenty grand's worth at five bucks a bill. That sets us back roughly a grand. They'll be here in the morning."

Chalice still brooded. "What's to stop him blowing the whistle on us even after he's paid? It's one of his specialties."

"You tell him that," I said. "You tell him that a compromise has to be worked out. That the money will be deposited in a bank somewhere so that we can't retrieve it. If we're still in circulation after the ball's over, Greasy gets the briefcase. Tell him he can be there to see the cash deposited. He'll go for it, Harry. I swear it!"

Chalice's sudden smile revealed most of his gold-filled teeth. "I think he will, mate. I honestly think he will! It's the sort of caper my old man used to pull at the fairgrounds. What happens when Greasy starts unloading this queer?"

Crying Eddie grinned. "You don't need no crystal ball to answer that one."

I shrugged a shoulder. "This stuff's good enough to get by a hotel cashier, a nightclub, or a bar, but the moment it hits a bank . . ." I made a plucking motion at the back of my collar.

The sound of Chalice rubbing his palms together was like sandpaper on wood.

"That's brains, you see, Ed. What they call strategy — the same as Rommel used. You set your trap and wait for the other geezer to walk into it."

Crying Eddie was inspecting a minute scratch on the back of a finger.

"You going to be here when Greasy shows up?"

"I can't be sure," I said vaguely. "By the way, you guys are going to have to get out of here between three and six this afternoon. There's a children's playground behind the Post Hotel. Take Sophie up there. The Baroness is paying me a visit."

Chalice's whistle was low and admiring. "And you only met her last night! I always thought them sort of birds didn't dabble."

Crying Eddie forgot the scratch in his distaste. "Dabble, mate! These people ain't even natural. I seen that Skomielna through the window this morning. Know what he was doing? He was sitting playing the pianner with a bleedin' wig on — in broad daylight!"

"He's eccentric," I said. "All you have to do is keep out of his reach. Did they send food up from the village?"

"Enough to feed a nick," said Chalice. "You must be spending a bomb of my money."

"Just getting in practice," I assured him. "Wait till you see me at work on my own. That'll really be something."

Sophie and I ate in the dining room. The maid was still in the house, so Chalice served the meal. He was getting quite professional. Sophie kept up a constant barrage of questions. Where was Eddie eating and why. Finally I had enough of it.

"Eddie's eating in the kitchen because it's the place for him to eat. And if you don't hush your mouth you're not going out with him this afternoon."

"Going out where?" she demanded, suspending her chewing. She had done her own hair that morning and the pigtails were uneven.

I finished my beer, making my voice airy. "Just a place that's specially built for kids with swings and carousels and goats pulling sleds. That's all."

She was down from her chair in a flash, her arms around me, and her lips tight against my cheek.

"I love you, Papa!"

That much she meant and no matter what happened I'd always have her. It's what you tell yourself at times like this.

Chalice and Crying took the car, giving the maid a lift downtown. The house was silent without them. I closed the curtains, replenished the fire, and burned some of Skomielna's essence on the logs. The big seduction scene was now set.

I was reared in the Ontario boondocks, where the Scots guard their customs and traditions jealously. Lamlash, Bruce County, has a pipe band, people still talk about 'the' porridge, and they eat it with salt. A Burns' night out there is no time or place for a Sassenach to be abroad. The only parent I even knew was my grandfather, a creaking giant of a man who remained the town's only doctor till the day he died. I've often wondered how he found the time to die. The Hendersons of his day were already fifth-generation Canadians and their mark was etched on a town they ruled ruthlessly. There was a Henderson Park, the Henderson Public Library, the Henderson Stove and Boiler factory. The town was part of the family and vice-versa. The itch to be remembered seemed to reach its apogee in the person of my grandfather.

Deserted by his son, as he sternly claimed, he threw himself into the duties of doctor, justice of the peace, elder of the Free Church of Scotland. Nobody in the great rambling house overlooking the lake ever mentioned my father and mother. It took me years to know that the truth was a simple story of rebellion. My father had come to his senses at the age of nineteen, packed a canvas bag one night, and sneaked out on the southbound. Six months later he married a Lithuanian lumberjack's daughter in Orchard, B.C. Another year and the bus they were traveling in to California took the wrong turn.

My grandfather traveled two thousand miles to bury them, returning with a month-old infant and a collection of dirty diapers. I grew up to enter ten schools in various parts of the world, emerging from each without either credit or gratitude. I beat my father's exit from Lamlash by a year. I was eighteen when I fled the town like a jail. One basic legacy of my upbringing was a strong sense of guilt in pleasure.

Right now, looking from the kitchen window, I felt as guilty as hell. Banked snow reflected the waning sunlight in the garden. I could hear the thud of stone from the curling rink, church bells reproving the returning skiers. It was twenty past three when Uschi's BMW nosed through the gates and up the slope. I hurried out to meet her. I had left the garage open, thinking she would want to park inside away from prying eyes. But she left her car outside and came into the house. The first thing she did was lock the door. The fire had climbed high in the massive chimney place. The long gracious room was quiet.

She dropped her car keys on the table, rid herself of the sealskin coat and hat, and shook her hair free. She was wearing a silk shirt and ski pants, no jewelry and no spectacles. She came toward me slowly, her hands by her side, looking directly into my eyes. She lifted her face to be kissed as I bent my head, then her arms cradled my neck. We must have stayed like that for fully a minute, our bodies straining together. I had to break away to retain my balance. She smiled and the image of a snow leopard came into my mind again. Every move she made was sure and feline. Even her voice was a purr as she took my hand.

"Lead me," she said. We walked upstairs, both of us looking straight ahead. I opened the door to my bedroom. The enormous gilt mirror trapped the light of the sinking sun. I took my clothes off in the dressing room, hurrying like a kid at the water hole. When I came back, she was sitting up in the swan bed, naked. Her hands were clasped behind her neck, her arms half-hidden by the cascade of oat-colored hair. The pose lifted magnificent breasts tipped with coral nipples. Her armpits were smooth dusky hollows.

"I want you, Paul," she said in a small distinct voice.

Arms and legs met mine, holding me in a vise as her tongue forced its way through my teeth. Her nails started to tattoo my back, like gentle needles at first and then more fiercely till the pain was intense. We were bound together now, rising and falling slowly, beyond care or reason. I've no idea how long it lasted, minutes, hours, an eternity. Suddenly I felt her body stiffen. I cried out loud as her teeth sank into my shoulder. I drove myself to the last shuddering end and found her mouth with mine. Her blue eyes were brilliant in the half-light. Sweat had made a tangle of the fine pale hair at her temples.

"You're mine," I said desperately. The words themselves meant nothing. What I was doing was saying thank-you to her for making me feel wanted.

She rolled sideways, reaching for her ski pants. She pulled a case and lighter from her pocket, lit two cigarettes, and gave me one. The stock gesture somehow disappointed me.

"Get me some water, darling, please."

I read once that there are two kinds of men. There are those who fetch water after making love and those to whom it is fetched. On this occasion I fetched. I came up the few steps from the bathroom, a towel decently draped around my middle. She took the glass from me and sipped, considering me over its rim. Her tone was honeyed with amusement.

"Thank you, Paul. I always wondered what it would be like to go to bed with a thief."

I was a yard or so from the bed at that moment. I froze there staring at her. It was some time before I could bring myself to speak and then only stupidly.

"What's that supposed to be — some sort of a joke?"

Inside my head I knew it was no joke. She put the glass down carefully on the bedside table.

"Oh, come on, Paul! I told myself that you'd be able to carry it off with style at least, don't disappoint me." She stretched out, reaching into her pants' pocket, and taking out a typewritten sheet of paper. She held this high in the air without opening it. "The whole thing's simple enough. I might not be over-imaginative but I do have a nose for the *louche*. You see, thieves have been trying to steal Marika's jewelry for the last twenty years. So the moment the insurance company knew that she was serious about her extravaganza, they insisted on special security precautions. They were the ones who suggested the Slade Agency. The agency provided me with a list of all the crooks who'd be likely to follow us to Todtsee. In some cases they supplied photographs. So the first thing that I did when Mischka telephoned was consult the list. And there you were, my sweet, under your own name, which seemed to me to be silly. But then I wouldn't know about these things."

Her naked body was suddenly repulsive and I looked away. She went on talking as calmly as a judge demonstrating a point of order. The paper was open now.

"'Paul Henderson, *alias* Alan Baillie. Aged thirty-eight.' You told me thirty-six! 'A record of one arrest in London, England, in October 1969. Henderson is a traveling thief known to be expert in the use of false keys and picklocks. Subject English. Fluent French and German, and poses as an archaeologist or grain broker. Six feet one, brown-gray hair, weight around 170 pounds, plausible manner.'"

She stuffed the paper back in her pants' pocket. "I don't mind the plausible manner in the least. It's cute."

I was too stunned to feel anything much but a sense of fear and failure. I kept thinking that here were guys like Chalice and Eddie who could go on pulling caper after caper without putting a foot wrong. Then I move in and the whole venture starts to fall apart. First Greasy George and now this blond bitch laughing at me. I retreated to the dressing room, not trusting myself to speak. I put my clothes on slowly, remembering the stupid boasts I'd made earlier — that the cops could do nothing, that we'd broken no law. The truth was, all the Baroness had to do was call police headquarters and a search would reveal the gas canisters stashed in the cellar, my burglar's kit, the false passports, and the guns I was sure the other two were carrying.

Uschi was fully dressed when I returned to the bedroom. She was sitting on a chair reading one of the magazines I'd bought earlier.

She tapped the cover with a scornful finger. "'*Nuits de Babylone*'! What rubbish these people print. I'm surprised you rely on gossip columns for information. I'd have thought you'd have better sources than that. Take this article, for instance. It says there are no less than four private detectives in the house constantly. They're wrong. There are nine."

The bed had been remade, the cover spread neatly across it. It was as if the scene of lust and passion existed only in my imagination. She jumped up, linking her arm in mine, and pulling me in front of the mirror.

"We *still* make a handsome couple, Paul. You need a drink, come downstairs."

We went down like that, arms locked like lovers. I was glad to be back in the drawing room. The shadows made it difficult to see her face. I poured myself a small glass of brandy.

"You think I've humiliated you, don't you?" she said shrewdly.

I was stiff and awkward, not caring too much what I said in answer.

"You must have some sort of a kink. You realize you acted like a whore?"

She tilted her head and laughed. Her poise was infuriating. "Because I went to bed with you? Nonsense. I don't do this sort of thing for a living if you're being literal. Anyway, I enjoyed it."

I moved a hand wearily. The brandy might as well have been water in my stomach.

"Look. I'll be out of here by morning if you want to give me till then."

She didn't appear to hear. "Is that child really your daughter?"

For some reason the question took me well below the belt and I flamed.

"She's my daughter. Why?"

She locked hands around a knee and leaned back looking at me through narrowed eyes.

"I'm thinking aloud, that's all. The two men with you are accomplices, of course?"

There seemed little sense in denying it. The question reminded me that they were probably fooling around with Sophie while Uschi tore the flesh from my bones. The line of memories formed on the right, each more disturbing than the last: Baxter and the waiting plane, Greasy George Gorbals — all the money that had already been spent on expenses. Morally I'd be obliged to repay my share of it.

"We'll be out of town by morning, all of us," I urged desperately.

She smoothed an eyebrow thoughtfully. "There were nearly fifty names on the list the Slade Agency supplied. Those two men don't appear on it as far as I can see, either by name or by description. Why is that if they're jewel thieves?"

"They're not jewel thieves," I said.

She frowned. "You just said they were — you said they were your accomplices."

"*You* said so," I answered. "They're my business partners."

She hunched over her knees, pensive for a moment. Then she pulled the piece of paper from her pocket and threw it into the fire.

"Now the agency men don't know that you exist. There was a copy file but I've destroyed that, too."

I watched the ashes crumble then float off, sucked by the draft in the chimney.

"Why would you do that?"

She rearranged her hair, stabbing some pins into it. "Because you're still going to steal Marika's jewelry. But with my help now." I looked at her dully.

"Well don't just sit there," she exclaimed. "Say something!"

It took some time for my brain to function. "Are you putting me on?" I demanded finally.

She moved her head swiftly. "I'm sick of poverty. It shouldn't be too difficult for you to understand. I've decided that we don't need your friends. You'll have to get rid of them."

I laughed outright, a hopeless sort of laugh that had nothing to do with humor.

"You don't know what you're saying. These aren't the sort of guys you just get rid of — even if I wanted to."

Her blue eyes flickered over me. She was as self-possessed as a headmistress addressing a P.T.A. meeting.

"It doesn't really matter, I suppose, as long as you make yourself responsible for them. But they'll have to do as they're told. What was your plan, Paul — how did you think of robbing Marika?"

All at once it seemed possible that she was really on the level. It was a slim hope that grew by the minute. I lit a cigarette.

"Well, we were going to cut the power line for a start."

She considered my answer seriously before deciding against it. "I don't believe you. How would you have been able to see yourselves? Were you going to use pistols?"

"No pistols."

"Then how?" There was the beginning of irritation in her

face. "You're professionals. You must have had some plan."

I moved my shoulder, reviving the pain where she had bit me. "We do, but you don't expect me to tell it to you, do you?"

She plucked my cigarette from between my fingers, took a couple of drags, and returned it.

"I expect you to answer *all* the questions I ask you, Paul. Let's be realistic about this, sweetheart. I can put the three of you in jail. Do you agree?"

I inspected the end of the butt. It was free of lipstick. "I'll give you that much, sure."

She ticked the statement off on a forefinger. "But I won't do it because I need you. Agreed again?"

"With reservations," I said. "You're asking me to help you steal your employer's property. Why couldn't I expose you?"

She lifted her chin, smiling. "Because I've hidden the real and horrible Uschi from my employer. Marika's heart is made of chromed steel but I'm as close to it as anyone is. She calls me her 'penniless little baroness' with a smile of affection. No, that wouldn't work, Paul. Why are we talking like this, anyway? We need one another."

There was a logic there that reminded me that I was in no position to play the clown. There were two courses open to us. Either we left town at speed or we stayed on her terms. I threw the cigarette end at the fireplace.

"You realize I'll have to talk it over with the others?"

She removed her teeth from the finger she'd been nibbling. "Do that. Tell them I want half the proceeds. Half for you and your friends and half for me."

I blinked hard, imagining the confusion *that* piece of news would cause. From my partners' point-of-view it was pre-

posterous enough being lumbered with an amateur confeder-
ate, a woman who had us by the short hairs, so to speak. And
on top of that, to have to agree to a straight split down the
middle. It was going to hurt.

"That's out of the question," I said impulsively. "They'll
never accept."

"If they're really professionals they will," she said coolly.
"Half of something is better than all of nothing."

This attitude of hers was beginning to get to me. Poised
on the edge of dangerous and alien territory, she was as self-
assured as a den mother at a cubs' clambake. But behind
the calmness was something else, an undertone of bitterness,
as if deep down she despised the world and herself with it.

"I wouldn't make book on that," I warned. "These guys
aren't a couple of neighborhood thugs. They're high-class
operators who don't even need the money."

"You're not going to tell me it's glory they want!" She
managed to make it sound ridiculous.

"Something like that," I agreed. "I'm different. I need the
money. Tell me something, Uschi. Have you any idea at all
just what it is you're getting yourself into?"

She had opened her purse and was using a comb. She
looked up from the tiny hand mirror.

"I think so, yes. God knows I've thought about it all for
long enough. What I don't know you'll have to tell me. Let
me ask you something, Paul. What do you think it takes to
make a thief? I mean, why do some people steal and others
don't?"

I spread my hands. "Some aren't afraid of the consequences — others are. Whether in the courts or in their con-
sciences. Some thieves justify their actions by saying that
they do no more than is done every day in big business. That

a holdup's no worse than one country's violation of another."

She pushed vaguely at a lock of hair that was in front of her eye. "That's not really an answer. Let me tell you a tale that's not very pretty. It might help you to understand me."

Her narrative was told unemotionally. It was that much more impressive because of it. I had the feeling that most of it at least was true. She'd been born in Estonia and had grown up in Poland, where her father was a high-ranking officer in the German army of occupation. She'd seen her parents' brains blown out by a liberator and had spent the next three years in an orphanage. An association for the care of officers' children had rescued her and sent her to a school near Baden. She stayed there till she was eighteen. It was the only home she had known. When she left, she was fluent in four languages, had a passport with her title on it, and two hundred and fifty dollars. She worked as a *vendeuse* on the rue du Faubourg-St.-Honoré, then as a film extra, and finally as secretary to a television producer in London. Marika Bergen had met her at a party and had promptly hired her. She told me without any sign of self-pity that she had never received a birthday present or held a man's love for longer than a couple of months.

"So you see," she finished, smiling now, "I take where I fancy when and if I can. There's no real difference between a woman like me and a man. We think about conquest and surrender in the same sort of way."

I found myself thinking about the long line of women I'd known but never understood. This one's approach was far easier.

"I can understand your bitterness," I said. "But to think the way you do, you must have had larceny in your heart from way back."

She put the mirror away and crossed her legs. "Maybe I did. Have you any idea what it's like to spend four years with someone like Marika Bergen? Can you imagine how it is to listen to her self-adulation for ten, twelve hours a day? She cares for nothing at all except herself and her money. There isn't a single one of her friends I haven't heard her seek to destroy or slander. There's no room in Marika's body for charity. For four long years she's insulted and humiliated me under the guise of being kind. I bided my time and now my chance has come."

I shifted my feet, eying her curiously. Much of what she said I could follow, but the tale had gaps like a horse's mouth.

"That file on me you burned," I said. "Remember how it described me — 'a traveling thief.' Well that's exactly what I am, Uschi. To be one and avoid unpleasant consequences you have to possess a certain expertise. You're risking your liberty, remember. Above all, unless you're working alone, you've got to have faith in your partners. And I'm not quite sure about you yet. There are times when you don't come on quite right. Like what you're saying about biding your time. Suppose I hadn't turned up?"

She made a move. "There'd have been someone else."

"With the ball no more than days away," I said with disbelief. "I know much more about this set-up than you give me credit for, Uschi. I know that the jewelry's only out of the vault for a week, for example. How can you talk about waiting for someone else?"

"When you've lived with a dream for as long as I have, it's bound to come true," she said confidently.

Basically, I guess, I wanted to believe her. It was less humiliating to be put through the hoops for a valid reason.

"Even a dream has to have shape," I reminded. "I'll go

along with the bit about waiting for your Prince Charming, but you must have had some definite role in mind for him. What was it?"

She smiled. "You'll see soon enough."

In a way she reminded me of Chalice. Both had the same sort of confidence that bordered on arrogance. I drew her attention again.

"You realize you're going to be a prominent suspect if this job is pulled? The town will look like an anthill with the top off."

The movement of her hand dismissed the suggestion. "I've thought about all that, naturally. But the police aren't magicians. What concerns me far more than that is how we dispose of Marika's jewelry. Nearly all of it is recognizable. Who would buy and who would have the money?"

It was satisfactory to know and to hint of superior knowledge. "That's one thing you needn't worry about. It's all taken care of. Let's get back to you. I've got to convince my partners that you're worth fifty per cent and . . ."

She stopped me in the middle of the sentence. "You don't have to convince them. They can take it or leave it."

"They just might leave it," I warned. "Don't ever lose sight of that. Then you and I are in trouble. We're the ones who really *need*. I want you to give me some ammunition for them."

She frowned. "Ammunition?"

"Information," I amended. "It would help if I could tell them where the jewelry's kept, for instance."

It was a couple of seconds before she replied. "In a safe in a room in Marika's suite. A detective watches it twenty-four hours a day. I'll have to go now, Paul. I'll phone tonight for your decision."

134

I stood up with her. "What decision?"

She shrugged into her coat, touching my cheek with a gesture that was becoming familiar.

"Your professional word, darling. Once I have that, we can start thinking of a plan."

"Once you have it," I corrected, "you have a plan as well."

I walked as far as her car. A cold wind chased the dead leaves over frozen grass. The glaciers on the sides of the mountains glittered in the shadows. She offered me her lips to be kissed.

"Good-bye, Paul. Remember, you need me much more than you need them. Try to make them understand that and be careful of Mischka. Whatever you do, be careful of Mischka."

It was a long lonely wait till I heard the Rolls draw up outside. Sophie was the first one in, hat off, pigtails flying. Her eyes were glowing and her nose pinched with cold. She grabbed me around the legs, bleating with excitement.

"I drove a sled, Papa. A sled with a goat in it!"

I patted the top of her head. "That's nice, sweetheart. Now go take your things off." She ran for the bedroom.

The other two flopped on the chairs before the fireplace. "Kids," said Chalice over his shoulder. "I don't know where they get their bleedin' energy. She fair wore me out." His bowler hat looked as if it had been used as a football.

I could just see Crying Eddie's legs protruding. His polished boots were impeccable. I had a sudden thought that he could have run a five-mile steeplechase and finished in the same condition. He made a bleating noise like a sheep.

"What do you know about kids, mate? At her age you was smoking cigars and playing poker."

The lights were out and my reflection in the gold-framed

mirror no more than a shadow as I moved in front of the fire.

"We've got trouble," I said.

They both straightened up in their seats. Chalice's back clicking in the process.

"You can't mean *more* trouble!" he said incredulously.

"The worst kind," I told him. "The Baroness is on to us. She knew who I was even before she came here last night."

Chalice rolled his eyes before closing them. "Jesus God!"

I tried to explain. "It's the detective agency and the insurance company between them. They've supplied her with files on all the likely customers. M.O.'s. Aliases. In some cases, pictures. What she had on me sounded as if it had been lifted straight from the Criminal Records Office."

"That does it . . ." Eddie started to say. Sophie's sudden appearance killed the conversation. She dragged one foot after another, looking in our direction. She hates isolation as nature abhors a vacuum. It was obvious that she thought she was missing something.

"What do you want?" I asked.

"Could I be a princess?" she demanded.

I turned her around and headed her toward the stone staircase. "I'd say that would be difficult but not impossible. Now you go on back to your room. If you're hungry, you can fix yourself something to eat. Turn the television on if you like. We're talking business."

Crying Eddie continued as soon as she had gone. "That's it, then, isn't it, Harry, mate? The sooner we're on that bleedin' plane the better."

Chalice was still sitting bolt upright. "Let's hear the rest of it, Paul."

136

I could hear music coming from Sophie's room. It seemed a long, long way away. I had difficulty in finding the right words.

"She came here to look us over. Don't laugh, but she's decided to rob Bergen of her jewelry. She needs professional assistance."

Chalice's heavy-lidded eyes shifted in my direction. "You're joking. What is she, some sort of nut?"

"She's a thief," I said. "Or that's what she wants to be. It's not too complicated when you hear her story." I gave it to them as it had come to me. "I wouldn't think she's kidding about a goddamn thing," I finished. "Let's look at the facts. We can get rid of the gas and my gear, anything that could make us hot. But you people came in on those phony p.p.'s. If she does turn us in, we're in trouble. Suppose we managed to straighten it out about the passports? That would still leave you x grand out of pocket for expenses. I'll level with you both. If that happens, I might as well start looking for a ditch-digging job. That's one side of it, now let's take the other. It isn't Bergen who runs Shahpur, it's the Baroness. With her behind us it's like planning to knock a bank over with the manager in on the deal. With her help we could make this caper one hundred per cent kosher. For that she wants a straight cut down the middle. Half for us and half for her. She's calling me tonight for an answer."

Chalice's voice sounded as if he were hollering through a bullhorn.

"*What!* You ain't being serious, are you, mate?"

I moved my head in assent. "Dead serious."

He looked at me as if snakes were crawling out of

my mouth. "We've been lumbered, Harry," Crying said bitterly. "I had a feeling in me water from the start and I was right. I told my old mum about it. Well and truly lumbered. This is like living in a madhouse and I'm getting out of it."

This was open mutiny and Chalice dealt with it promptly. He was out of his seat before I could shift my weight from one foot to the other. He grabbed Crying Eddie's tie, bunched it in his fist, and brought the whole thing up under his partner's chin. Eddie was on his toes with his shoulder blades against the chairback.

"You ain't going nowhere," snarled Chalice. "Not without I say so. Now sit still and belt up."

Dust flew as he threw Crying back in the chair. Eddie ran his fingers over his throat, eying me meanly. I could feel the knife in his mind sink deep into my belly. I lit a cigarette. I'd no idea anymore how many I was getting through in a day.

Chalice's voice was under control again. "One question, Paul. Did you have it off with her or not?"

I wriggled my shoulders. "I did. As soon as we'd finished in bed she pulled my file out of her pants' pocket and read it to me."

His face wrinkled into a smile of delight. "I'd have paid money to see that."

The memory was still humiliating. "You're paying," I said shortly.

His eyes and mouth were sober again. "How do you feel about her now?"

I flicked ash behind me. "*Feel* about her? I'm not too sure that I understand you."

138

He knuckled the top of his scalp, watching me carefully all the while.

"I want to know whether you trust her."

I had been thinking about it ever since she had left the house. "She's tricky but I think we can handle her."

"So you say stay, right?" asked Chalice. I nodded. He shifted his gaze. "How about you, Ed?"

Crying hadn't spoken since Chalice jumped him. His voice was charged with resentment.

"What's it matter what I think?"

"We'll take that as meaning no," Chalice said composedly. "One no and one yes, so it's up to me. I say we stay so you're outvoted, Ed. O.K.?"

The younger man took defeat the hard way, his eyes and mouth taut.

"It's got to be O.K., hasn't it? Why don't you ask if this bird's got a file on us, too?"

"Has she?" said Chalice.

"No," I admitted. "But she knows we're together. I said as much. She'd have guessed in any case. She's not interested in either of you two, anyway. As a matter of fact she'd like to get rid of you."

"Would she now!" Chalice remarked with interest. I guessed that his devious brain was already exploring the possibilities of Uschi's stand. His next words proved me right. "Suppose she's setting us up for something, Paul."

That too I had thought about. I kicked the logs to a blaze. Their faces were ruddy in the sudden light, Chalice's thoughtful, his partner's sullen. I opened the drinks cupboard and poured two Scotches. I gave one to Chalice.

"I'd put nothing past her, but in this case she'd have no

motive. As Baroness von und zu Regensdorf she comes on loud and clear but as an operator she's nowhere. Sure she knows what Bergen's gear is worth — or what it's insured for, rather. But she doesn't know where to sell it. The only thing she's got going for her in this setup is an inside berth. That and the larceny in her heart. She hasn't even got a plan and she certainly can't guess that we're going to clean the whole goddamn house. No, Harry, I can't see a cross. She needs us too much for that."

"Then you haven't told her about the gas?"

"Of course not. We'll have to decide about that when the time comes. Make no mistakes about her. She's smart and she'll learn fast. The thing to do is to let her think she's using us while we use her."

Eddie's arm came up in the manner of a small boy asking to leave the room.

"Is it all right if I say something?"

"We can't stop you," Chalice said wearily.

"Thank you," said Crying. "I think you're both talking like a pair of jerks. This woman is a menace but I don't see why you take her so seriously. O.K., so she thinks she's going to get fifty per cent. Make it seventy-five if she likes. The truth is, of course, she won't get a bleedin' penny."

I put my empty glass down carefully. "I've got a strong feeling that she's taking that possibility into consideration. I told you she's smart. She's going to be watching me closely."

Crying Eddie leaked a sarcastic smile from the corner of his mouth. There was no doubt about his meaning.

"Then I would say she's smart. Watching you closely's what we all ought to do."

I was on my feet at the same time as he was, the difference in years forgotten. The only thought in my head was to smash the sneer into the back of Crying's skull. Chalice slipped between us quickly, blocking our swinging arms. His shove sent his partner reeling. Crying Eddie shook himself like a wet dog.

"That's the second time tonight, Ed," warned Chalice. "Let's not have a third. Fuck off!"

I heard the kitchen door slam behind Crying. Chalice straightened his coat. "He don't mean it, Paul. It's just that he's up tight. He's always like this before we make a hit."

I rubbed my biceps where his fingers had dug in. "I've taken all I can, Harry. Just keep him off my back. Do you want me to be here when Greasy shows up?"

He collected the two empty glasses. "Not if you've got something better to do."

I threw some logs on the fire, speaking with my back to him. "I'll wait for the Baroness to call, then I'm going out. Don't wait up for me. I don't know how long I'll be." I could feel his eyes with my shoulder blades. "I'm going up to Shahpur. I'm taking nothing on trust anymore. I'm casing the place tonight."

He peered at me as if seeing something completely lost to my own eyes.

"Be lucky, mate."

I looked in at Sophie. She'd fixed herself a sandwich. The remains of it and a glass that had held milk were on the table beside her bed. The television set was switched off. She was lying on her stomach again. I turned her over gently. She sighed complainingly, opened her eyes in a stare of bewilderment, and was asleep again. Mine, I thought, putting the covers over her. There was nothing anyone could do to change that.

I sat upstairs in my bedroom, waiting for Uschi's call. The window framed a sliver of moon that was lying on its back. Down in the village below, the lamps seemed to be burning with extravagant brightness. I sat on the bed, thinking about Marika Bergen's guests who'd be starting their dinners about now, oblivious to the fate that was being planned for them. The thought took me back to Uschi inevitably. For years I'd just done things my way without trying to justify what I did or having any moral qualms about it. Now chance had planted Uschi squarely in my lap. In some ways we were much alike. We were both outlaws by nature. Both of us needed this one big chance to cross over on the sunny side of the street. We'd both waited for it. I found myself remembering her cold Baltic stare and the warmth of her body — the hungriness of her passion — the way she'd tricked me with it almost contemptuously. The memory left me with a twinge of uneasiness. I could well understand that for Chalice and Crying she was no more than an unwelcome hitchhiker to be dumped at the end of the ride. What I couldn't understand was my own reluctance to write her off. By all the rules of the game I should have been more hostile than either of the others, yet I made excuses for her. It was a disquieting reflection.

I dressed in the darkest clothes I had with me, putting on foam rubber shoes and a dark-blue flannel shirt. I took no hat, aware that my ears would probably drop off, but a hat is too easily lost in a scramble for safety. It was a half-hour before Uschi's call came through. She spoke in a throaty whisper.

142

"I can't stay long. People are here. Have you made up your minds?"

I could hear the background noises of a party going on, the tinkle of glass, laughter, voices.

"We're in," I said. "All of us. The answer's yes."

"I must go," she said quickly. "I'll try to see you tomorrow afternoon again. I'll let you know in the morning." She blew a kiss down the line and hung up.

I collected my tools from the cellar and peeked around the kitchen door. The room pulsated with heat. A round of Stilton cheese stood on the table where Chalice and Crying were playing their Chinese checkers. There were wedges of bread and butter on a plate and a tall glass of beer for Chalice.

"I'm splitting," I announced. "One of you look in on Sophie before you go to bed."

Crying Eddie kept his eyes on the checkerboard but Chalice looked up.

"All right, mate. Look after yourself."

I'd intended to walk down to the village. There was time to kill and I wanted to be alone. But halfway down to the gates head lamps lit the garden. The Porsche clattered out of the garage and stopped abreast of me. Skomielna wound down the window.

"My dear fellow, you're not walking *again!* In this weather and with no hat?"

As far as I was concerned he was still across the valley with Bergen. I hadn't even heard the Porsche return. He was wearing a frogged coat that reached to his ankles and a Cossack cap.

"I need the exercise," I said lamely.

"Absolute nonsense," he answered, and opened the door.

"I insist on giving you a lift, Paul. Where are you bound for?"

I took the seat beside him. His eyes were fogged and he smelled heavily of vodka.

"You can drop me off at the Palace," I said.

He rammed the stubby gearshift into low. "I'm *exhausted*, literally exhausted. I've been with the Snow Queen all day. I only came back for some drawings. Have you seen Uschi again?"

He sounded no more than mildly curious but I was on my guard. "I saw her this morning for a drink." I didn't elaborate.

I thought he'd go on from there — had she said anything more about my invitation — had there been any mention of money — but he dropped the subject completely.

He used his brakes as if he were driving over a rock-hard stretch of highway. The resulting skid carried us barely wide of a gatepost. He corrected the skid with a flourish of the wheel.

"You can't *imagine* the problems I'm having with Marika. Her costume arrived from Givenchy. Now I ask you, Paul. A Watteau shepherdess at her age! And we're all supposed to go into transports about it. There's one blessing. We're not going to have to sit in that *freezing* stadium and listen to Berlioz."

The car was bucking like a mustang. I was desperately hanging on to the door.

"You mean she's not going to skate."

He hiccoughed loudly. "Canceled, poor dear. She fell on her little rubadub this morning. Wrong music, of course."

A solid white line appeared in the center of the road before us, shining through the hardening slush. Skomielna maneuvered the wheel so that the Porsche straddled the line. He smiled like an ancient satyr.

"Don't be frightened, dear boy. I *always* see two lines after eight o'clock at night. So I keep one wheel in the middle of them for safety." He took the last bend as though he was driving a bobsled and came off the banked snow in a sliding curve. I braced myself, shoving my knees against the dashboard, and waited for the inevitable crash. But somehow we were on the flat and safe.

"Hold it," I said firmly.

He braked hard. I removed my nose from the windshield. "You can let me off here," I said. I found the ground with my feet and stood up.

The shock of our sudden halt had left his Cossack cap tilted at a rakish angle. He winked with a sort of pleased maliciousness. "Don't neglect Uschi. Strike while the iron is hot. I can tell that she's taken with you. And by the way, don't forget our little arrangement."

"I won't forget," I promised, "and thanks for the lift." The Porsche roared away, spattering the sidewalk with slush. I walked downtown, taking my time. The bars and *boîtes* open and close early in Todtsee. I toured the better ones for the next couple of hours, drinking tonic water. Bergen's guests were everywhere. I recognized face after face from the glossies and gossip columns. Their voices were always a little louder than those of others. They posed, pouting and scowling, to the popping of photographers' flashbulbs. The women's clothes bore the cachets of St. Laurent and Carven, long dresses with plunging necklines, velvet throat bands studded with jewels, trouser suits tailored in expensive fabrics. The men were no less flamboyant with Regency shirts, velvet pants, and buckled shoes. They were all so very sure of themselves and their world — sure that tomorrow would be exactly the same as today and their places in it secure.

I called the airfield from the King's Bar and had Baxter on the line right away. He was sober and respectful. I elaborated some on the Tokyo story, saying that my associates were still held up in Japan. I'd keep him informed. It was midnight when I went out to the street. I shoved my hands deep in my pockets and started walking up the steep slope. It took me twenty minutes to reach the plateau where Shahpur was built. The house was a rambling mansion with separate quarters for the servants. According to what I'd read, these had once been the women's apartments. Empty during the war years, Shahpur had been rented successively by a Dutch margarine manufacturer and by the last of the Hollywood sweethearts. Every account spoke of the richness of its interiors, the Oriental carpets, copper-gilt and bronze censers. There was enough Indian and Tibetan sculpture to stock a museum, a heated swimming pool, a squash court, and a polo field.

I was out of breath when I reached the tall brick wall topped with revolving spikes. The village lay directly beneath me. The sliver of moon had climbed higher. Lights shone in the entrance lodge. It took me a good quarter-hour to make a circuit of the forbidding wall. Snow slid from the top as I passed, powdering my face and neck. I could see nothing that would serve as an aid to negotiate the wall — no tree nearby, no building — nothing but an expanse of silent snow with telephone poles sticking out of it. The only way into the estate was either through or over the ornate gates facing me. A driveway beyond curved into the trees and darkness. The snow there was crisscrossed with tire tracks and footsteps. I tried the gates with gloved fingers. They were locked securely. I crept over to a curtained window in the outside wall of the lodge and peeped through a chink in the curtain. A large grizzled head showed over the top of an armchair. Its owner was sitting in front of a television set, beating time to the polka music.

I hauled myself up on the gate, straddled the top, and dropped down on the far side. I waited there for a second, crouched, ready for a sign of alarm from the lodge. There was nothing but the muffled sound of the accordions. I trotted up the driveway between trees that gradually took on substance. They were tall and heavy with snow, standing back at the end and where they ringed the concourse in front of the two-story mansion. The number of lights burning surprised me. They seemed to be everywhere, behind curtains, in shutterless windows, on outside walls. The steps leading up to the massive door were illuminated by a high-powered lantern. In spite of the well-lit façade there was no sound anywhere. It was as if the whole household had frozen with my first step onto the property and was waiting for my next move before exploding into action. There was no chance even of approaching any of the windows without etching footmarks in the snow-covered flower beds. A central cupola bulged above the ballroom. Two wings, both a good thirty yards long, extended on each side. A plow had cleared the concourse down to the gravel, leaving ridges of snow around the perimeter. A path had been cut around the end of the east wing. I followed it to the back of the house. The lighting there was as brilliant as in front. As I reached a yard in front of the garage, I had my first glimpse of movement. A woman in maid's uniform appeared behind one of the kitchen windows. I inched along the wall opposite till I felt a gap open on my right. An oily-smelling darkness extended behind me. Chrome glimmered on the parked cars. The weighted door hung above my head.

Everything was true to the architect's drawings. The squash court had to be overhead. I could see the covered way leading from the kitchen area to the servants' quarters. The polo field was at the far end of the opposite wing. I stood shivering, listening to the sound of a clock chiming down in the village. The mournful tolling depressed me. Cold had invaded my wrists and ankles, and my eyes and nose were watering. I found myself wondering what they'd do with Sophie if I got busted. Imagination had taken me as far as a sanitary Swiss refuge for children, when a noise turned my head. A door opened in the covered passage, the angle of light gradually widening till a man's body was revealed. A shoulder holster was buckled over his bulky sweater. His head came out cautiously like a tortoise investigating a lettuce patch. It was one of the cops I had seen at the stadium. He hawked, spat and shivered, then called to someone inside.

"It'd freeze your goddamn balls off out there, Charley." He slammed the door shut.

There are times when you can sense with certainty what is going to happen. I knew instinctively that the door would be left unlocked. All the windows across the yard were heavily barred. I could hear women's voices behind the chintz curtains, two or three of them now. I tiptoed across the yard, keeping to the shadow. The door handle opened easily. I stepped into a corridor lit by overhead lights. A pair of overshoes stood on the linoleum just inside the door. There was a strong smell of ham frying. I shut the door quietly behind me and stood there listening. All I could hear was the banging of my heart in its rib cage. A right turn would take me to where the servants slept. Left took me to the house. I already knew that there was no way off the property except through the lodge gates. I needed to know the inside of the house — to engrave it on my brain till I could *feel* my way to freedom if necessary. I moved toward the kitchen. Six paces; stop, head cocked; and then forward again.

I'd gone maybe twenty feet like this when I heard someone coming in my direction. I stepped through the nearest door, my brain retaining a memory of the marks my wet shoes had left on the floor. The broom closet smelled of floor wax. The footsteps passed the closet and stopped at the door to the yard. I expected the man to open it and start his outside rounds, but he was back again almost immediately. His slow tread died away again in the direction from which he had come. I waited a few minutes and then opened the closet door a fraction. The corridor lights had been extinguished. I felt my way back to the yard door. The bolts were shut, the door locked, and the key gone. I checked my watch. Twenty-five minutes to one.

The first feeling of panic fluttered in my stomach. Moonlight shafted through the barred windows of the kitchen. I tried the door there, a cat curled on a chair watching me curiously. Locked as well, no key in sight. The corridor made a right angle. A couple of yards after the turn, light shone through an open doorway. I stole nearer. The room was empty. There was a desk, some deep-seated chairs, three telephones, one of them colored red. The ashtray was full of dead butts, and tobacco smoke still hung in the air. On top of the desk was a board with a duty roster clipped to it.

SLADE SECURITY SERVICE

Miss Bergen's Suite:	12 P.M.–8	P.M.	CALLAGHAN
	8 P.M.–4	A.M.	SHARP
	4 A.M.–12	P.M.	WINOGRADSKY
Relief:	MCKIE		
General Duties:	12 P.M.–8	P.M.	SCHULBERG
	8 P.M.–4	A.M.	TRACY
	4 A.M.–12	P.M.	DISTEFANI
Reliefs:	GOSS, PILIT		

A card was tucked into the bottom of the red phone: FEDERAL POLICE. There was no dial as on the others. The roster told me that there were at least two men around, possibly three. I couldn't be sure where the reliefs were located. I settled myself back in the broom closet to give the outside patrols time to move on their rounds. The minutes ticked away slowly till I heard the same footsteps. The same slow tread passed, the back door was tried. The cat yowled as if it had been booted, then there was silence. I stepped out into the corridor. Green baize doors twenty feet apart protected the main area of the house from the sounds and smells of the kitchen area.

I pushed the first one back with a sense of having done it all before. Everything I had read about Shahpur was clear-cut in my memory. A cork-lined door on my right opened into the furnace room. The walls were plain brick, the floor paved with asbestos. An oil-fired burner hummed in the center of the room, causing the air to vibrate. The heating system was automatic. Needles quivered on half a dozen gauges. Through an archway was the air-conditioning unit. I could see the two inspection plates, one on each side of the ducts that rose, crossed the ceiling, and disappeared in the thickness of the wall. This was virtually the nerve center of the house: the main fuse box was here, the telephone cables, the water valves. An unstapled cord dangled with the other phone lines. Almost certainly it connected the red phone I had seen with the police station.

I pushed the second baize door and found myself in the main entrance hall. A matching pair of staircases spiraled up to an overhead gallery. A few lights burned discreetly. The rest had been extinguished. Mirrors in the hall reflected jade carvings of Mongolian ponies, a black stone head of Shiva. A clock ticked steadily somewhere out of sight. The glass doors to the ballroom were on my right. I crossed the hall to the front door. Two locks secured it, one a spring type, the other a mortise. Only the spring lock was in use. I opened the door a fraction. The one light still burning came from the lantern overhead. I pulled the door after me and ran hard for the shelter of the fir trees. A flickering light appeared as I reached them. It was coming from the direction of the garage. Someone was using a flashlight. The beam hit the row of windows on the second story, settling on each ledge for a second like a moth. It was my friend from the stadium again, wearing a checked cap with his mackinaw. The flashlight was in his left hand, his right held a police special. He walked up the steps, took one last look at the garden, then let himself into the house. The bolts rattled home.

The lodge was in darkness when I reached it. I climbed

over the gates and hurried down the hill without looking back. The big clock outside the railroad station said ten minutes after one. I hailed a droshky driver coming out of the square. He reined the blanketed gray back on its haunches, peering down over a red, veined nose. I told him where I wanted to go. He mumbled something about it being late and demanded an outrageous fare. I wrapped myself in the moth-eaten bear robe, too cold to even light a cigarette, too drained mentally to think properly. We clipclopped up through narrow streets where neon signs blinked on empty sidewalks. Lights still blazed in the bigger hotels. I shut my eyes and kept them shut till we reached the house. The Porsche was parked where Skomielna had skidded to a halt, broadside across the garage entrance.

I locked the door and brewed myself a cup of coffee. After a while I dragged myself through the silent rooms and put my burglar's kit back in its hiding place. A toothpick would have been as much use. Chalice's door was ajar. The light snapped on as I passed. He was sitting up in bed, hugging his knees.

"I was beginning to think you'd come unstuck. What kept you?"

I propped myself against the doorway, too tired to stand up properly.

"What did you expect, a carrier pigeon? I was as fast as I could be."

Crying Eddie was snoring steadily. Chalice's face signified despair as he looked at his partner.

"Greasy George showed. The bastard's got more nerve than me and you put together, mate. It makes me want to throw up just being in the same room with him."

I nodded wearily. "So?"

He swallowed another yawn. "There was a few hard words at the beginning. I done what you said and lost me temper into the bargain. He's a smooth article, I'll say that for him. He just sat in the chair, listening like a bishop in a whorehouse. You've got to meet him tomorrow at twelve noon sharp. Where you were today. He says you'll know. And he'll choose his own bank. How'd you go, mate?"

There was no point in advertising the luck I'd had. "I made out. I was a good hour inside the house. I've located the power lines, the phone cables — everything. The air-conditioning unit's just as you said it was."

Chalice aimed a shoe at the other bed. The snoring subsided. "Terrific. Is that bird coming here again tomorrow?"

I took my shoulder off the door frame. "I'd say yes. I'll know in the morning for sure. Why don't you all go for a joyride? Get Baxter to fly you somewhere. Sophie'd like it. Bergen's canceled the skating, by the way. Skomielna told me."

He nestled back in the pillows. "Good night, mate. We're going to make this score."

"I know it," I answered. "And the Baroness knows it, too. I'll leave you with that small thought to consider. G'night."

I dreamt that I was in this cell, sentenced to life imprisonment. The windows overhead were barred and out of reach. I kept walking up and down, hearing people on the street outside. Suddenly somebody laughed and the footsteps dwindled into nothing. There was a pile of foolscap and a pen on the table. I sat down and started to write my good-bye-forever letters.

Chapter Five

AN INSISTENT TUGGING rescued me from the nightmare. I opened one eye after another and saw my daughter. A sporty yellow sweater topped her minute ski pants. She'd managed to get her hair into an elastic band. Her blond tresses swung in a ponytail. She had carried up a tray with toast, tea, and orange juice. She deposited it in my lap, concentrating with her tongue, her eyes somewhat unfriendly.

"I was thirsty during the night and called you. Eddie came." She managed to capsule treachery and heartbreak into the brief statement.

I struggled up, lifting the cup with unsteady fingers. The five peaks beyond the bathroom windows were jagged against a washed-blue sky. The stretches of snow between the pines dazzled my eyes. She picked up my clothes from the floor and put them on a chair. She returned to her theme deliberately.

"Why didn't you come, Papa?"

My watch said twenty after nine. I could hear the radio downstairs playing the martial music Chalice favors in the morning. I answered through a mouthful of toast.

"I had to go out, sweetie pie."

She wormed her way a little nearer. "I saw the Prince this morning."

"That's nice," I said mechanically. The strong tea had cleared away the taste of sleep.

She wasn't going to be sidetracked. "Where did you *go*, Papa?"

I put the tray on the table beside me. "Now look, honey, I said I had to go out."

She stared at me from the bottom of the bed. "I'm not going to school, you know."

"Who in hell said anything about school?" I demanded. "I told you we're going to get you a governess."

She twined her legs. "What's a governess?" This sort of thing can go on for hours unless it's broken up.

"Someone who'll teach you to read."

"I *can* read," she said in a small distinct voice.

I pulled her up on the bed beside me. "Now listen to me, honey. Remember that house in the country — the one with the lollipop trees and Bumpy, the pony?" The fantasy was chock-a-block with everything we both longed for. I swear to goodness neither of us was likely to forget a single detail. She lifted her head and nodded. "O.K.," I said. "Well, pretty soon we're going to be there. Now get out of here and let me take a bath."

She slid down to the floor and stood there for a second, looking up at me. If I'd sprouted another head she'd have loved me just the same.

I showered and called the airfield. Baxter brightened when I told him what I had in mind. It seemed that he'd exhausted all the possibilities of excitement in the building. He'd loop the party, he said, wherever I wanted. I left the details to him. The margins of time were narrowing. Only thirty-six hours were left till the ball. The thermometer outside the bathroom window gave a reading of minus twelve degrees Centigrade. Uschi's call came through as I was finishing dressing. She was coming to the house at the same time as yesterday. I found Chalice in an apron, polishing silver. Eddie was writing a postcard in a script that was surprisingly beautiful. Sophie was at his side, watching.

"Right," I said breezily. "You people take the car and have lunch in the village. Make a day of it. After lunch you can drive out to the airfield. Ask at the Swissair desk for Captain Baxter."

I hadn't expected the news to cause a sensation but there was a curious lack of enthusiasm on their faces. I looked down at my clothing, thinking for a moment that I had forgotten something. Chalice's chin jerked in the direction of the guesthouse. He closed the eye on Sophie's blind side.

"We just had a visitor."

I did a double take. The kitchen clock showed the same time as my watch. Twenty minutes to ten.

"His conscience must be troubling him," I said. Chalice's look told me to be careful. I shooed Sophie to the door and told her to go make her bed. "O.K.," I said. "What's going on?"

He handed me an envelope. "He left this for you."

I ripped the envelope open. A single piece of paper was inside. On it was a scrawled message: *O tra-la-la-la, Monsieur Henderson!* I read it over twice, once silently and once aloud, shaking my head.

"The guy's a nut."

"It's Sophie," said Chalice. "She told him your girl friend had been here — or as good as."

I stared through the window. Scraps of food were frozen into the snow. A ratty-looking jackdaw was removing them with surgical precision. I threw the note into the garbage pail.

"What's the matter with me — don't I live right or something! You must have heard what was being said. Why didn't one of you stop her?"

Crying Eddie's small flat ears moved in unison with his jaw muscles.

"Because we know our place, mate. She was upstairs and we was down here."

Chalice shifted his legs and threw his apron at the sink. He pointed at a gilt lipstick holder winking in the sunshine.

"She'd been playing with that bleedin' thing all morning. She told him where she found it — in your bedroom."

"What did he say?" I demanded.

He stacked the silver on the table. "Nothing. He just went to the desk, wrote that note, and told me to give it to you."

There was nothing to be done about it. Five minutes afterward, the house was empty except for the maid and me. By the time I'd walked downtown the post office was already crowded. I joined the queue waiting at the *poste restante* counter. A clerk there exchanged a package for a peek at my passport. The paper that had been used was the kind employed in gift wrapping. There was no one on the square in front of the *Kursaal* except an old man bundled in a blanket. I sat in front of a statue of William Tell and tore the package open. The return address written on the wrapping paper was a false one. The forged bills were in a shoe box. They looked right and felt right. Someone had put them through a tumbling machine, leaving them creased as if from use and here and there discolored. A Scotty Dundas refinement was the odd bill that bore scribbled digits such as cashiers use. I bought a dispatch case in a nearby store and stuffed the bills into it. I walked into the Gambrinus at twelve noon precisely. Greasy George was sitting at the table at the bottom of the stairs. A black Homburg and dark overcoat gave him a faintly clerical appearance. He smiled benevolently as he saw me.

"Got everything with you?" he inquired.

I put the dispatch case down between us. The waiter brought me a coffee and returned to his post. I spooned sugar into the cup, looking at the venerable head across the table.

"A thieves' pimp," I said bitterly. "Where does a guy go from there — I wonder you can live with yourself!"

His answer was a hearty laugh, snake's eyes disappearing in creases of fat.

"You got a real sense of humor, Henderson. I like you. Is this it?" He tapped the handle of the case on the table.

I nodded. He consulted an old-fashioned watch. "They're expecting us at the bank. I'm Mr. Brown, you're Mr. Smith. I think I'll take a look inside this before we go."

"I'll be sitting right here," I replied. "And there's only one way out of the place."

"A real joker," he said, heaving himself up on his feet and taking the case. "Buy yourself another cup of coffee." He vanished into the men's room. Time dragged by. I wasn't worried. It was going to take far more than a casual check to detect the fact that the bills were forged. The discrepancies were minute — a slight blurring of color — a digit out of line. He came back and gave me the bag.

"You finally rowed yourself in with a good team, did you, mate? Good on yer. Let's get going."

We walked a couple of hundred yards to a glass-and-steel building in the modern Swiss manner. Outside the entrance was a bronze name plate.

BANK LEOPOLD

KASSE & BÜRO

3 STOCK

The elevator whispered its way up to the third floor, Greasy George looking into his hat thoughtfully. The small private bank occupied the whole floor. A girl showed us into a waiting room where a TV screen relayed the latest stock movements from the Zürich market. The door was thrown open abruptly by a bony man dressed in gray.

"Vice-President Mayer," he said in English, and bowed. "Mr. Brown?" he inquired, looking at each of us with humorless spectacled eyes.

Greasy George bowed in turn. "I'm Mr. Brown. As I told you on the telephone, Mr. Smith and I have a business arrangement which requires this case to be deposited with your bank."

No Swiss banker worthy of the name has been known to show surprise at any arrangement that involves the acquisition of money, even temporarily. Mayer was no exception to the rule. He sat down, unscrewed the top of a gold fountain pen, and squared his shoulders.

"Now, gentlemen, do you wish to disclose the nature of the contents of this bag or not?"

Greasy George smiled at me. "We do indeed. It contains twenty thousand dollars in United States currency." He shoved the bag across the table.

The move took me completely by surprise. I'd counted on

George's inspection but certainly not on a banker's. Mayer riffed through the banded bills, one finger jerking like the needle on a sewing machine. Suddenly he stopped dead, frowning. I held my breath but it was no more than a miscount. He licked his finger and continued. He stacked the bills back in the dispatch case and put a seal over the lock.

"Twenty thousand dollars is correct, gentlemen."

It was as if he had waved a wand and given the phony bills respectability. Greasy George was throaty with pleasure.

"The bag and contents are to be released to me without further ceremony forty-eight hours from now, Mr. Mayer."

The banker queried the statement with me and I signified approval.

"I'm only acting as an agent, you understand. My instructions are to deliver this money and agree to these conditions."

The banker made a note of the time and rose. "If you gentlemen don't mind waiting for a minute, I'll have a form of release drawn up. The money will be placed in the vaults exactly as it is."

"Fine," said Greasy. "I'll be making a deposit in due course, naturally."

The door closed on Mayer. We sat there watching the Telexed figures jumping on the screen. Greasy George's air was that of a man familiar with such matters. Mayer returned with a typed form for me to sign. My scrawl was indecipherable. The banker came as far as the elevators with us. George and I parted in the hall downstairs.

"So long, mate," he smiled. "Give my regards to those clowns up on the hill and don't fall over your feet tomorrow night."

He waddled away up Bahnhofstrasse and made a right turn. I went left to the Palace Hotel. The bar was crowded with people I'd seen the night before. The refugees from Estoril and Acapulco moved among the ordinary tourists like birds of paradise negotiating a barnyard. I ate a sandwich and drank a Carlsberg, telling myself that there was nothing more to be done about George. One thing was certain — I dared not risk telling Uschi that a professional extortioner and police informer was on our tail. The news would surely stampede her.

I was home shortly before three and stopped a minute in the garden, looking down at the village. The plumes of smoke rose straight as arrows in the waning sunlight. I thought about the home Sophie and I were going to have — somewhere in France, maybe, in the foothills of the western Pyrénées. I had a vision of a countryside where axes rang among giant oak trees, of lush mountain pastureland with sleek oxen and a few blood horses. There'd be a timbered house behind a high stone wall and beyond that a forest that would be ours. The trouble was that an irritating presence cat-footed around in my dream croaking, *Beware*.

The drawing room lay in a golden light. The maid had re-filled the bowl of potpourri. I was sick of the face that met me in the mirror. Sick of the scowl that had become ritual, of the scarred nose, of the two teeth that needed capping. I kicked the fire to a crackling blaze and pulled a chair out of the sunlight. A picture of one of Skomielna's ancestors watched me sardonically, as if he too had done all this before and found it not worth the trouble.

I heard Uschi's car turn in through the gates and reached the door at the same time as she did. She was wearing her gray sealskin coat and matching hat. She threw them on a chair and threaded her arm through mine like an old and trusted comrade. Her hair was coiled low on the back of her neck and there were gold hoops in her ears. She pulled me down on the sofa beside her.

"Every time I leave you, you change, Paul. What *happens* in between?"

I moved a defensive shoulder. "I'm a worrier. Look, there's a lot to be settled and we're running out of time. Let's stick to business for the moment."

Her eyes widened and then she smiled. "You know, darling, I don't think you really understand me. You are just as important to me as business. We're going to *share* something, Paul. I meant what I said. It doesn't matter if it lasts six months, five years, or eternity just as long as it's real. Don't you see that?"

A remembered fragrance of burning leaves drifted into the house. I was playing a game within a game and making up two sets of rules as I went.

"I'll tell you what I see," I said heavily. "I see one of us turning into the Old Man of the Sea. Have you thought of that?"

She touched her hair, her blue silk sleeve rustling like a live thing.

"As a matter of fact, I have. I spent the best part of last night thinking about it. I decided that the risk was worth running. You see, in a limited way I love you."

I started to laugh. It wasn't just the words, it was the camp way in which she said them. After a moment's indecision she started laughing with me. It was one of those contagious affairs where a grimace or giggle can start the whole thing over again. It was a while before we managed to get a hold on ourselves. I wiped my eyes with my handkerchief. My defenses were still up, but I realized that she'd gotten her foot through the crack in the door.

"Skomielna knows," I said soberly.

It was the first time I had seen even the hint of fear in her eyes. Her chin came up slowly.

"Knows what — who you are?"

I moved my head rapidly. "You left your lipstick in my bedroom. Sophie found it and told him. You know the way kids are."

She nibbled on a cuticle and then shrugged. "The trouble is that he spends most of the day with Marika. Ah well, it can't be helped, I suppose. Anyway, he's been so malicious with his tongue for the past week, she no longer believes a word that he says."

We sat for a while, thinking our own thoughts like strangers in a doctor's waiting room. Her eyes were serious when she spoke.

"There are only thirty-six hours left, Paul. I have to know your plan."

I'd considered how I would tell it, figuring that I'd trade confidence for confidence till I was completely sure of her. One thing was uppermost in my mind. For the time being at least, the big card was hers.

"Settle down and don't rush your fences," I said. "First tell me about the house. I want to know where people sleep, how the cops operate."

She brought her long legs together, staring down at them as I touched flame to her cigarette. Her description matched what I had seen precisely.

"There's an air-conditioning system, isn't there?" I prompted when she was done.

She looked at me, puzzled. For the first time I noticed that she smoked without inhaling.

"An air-conditioning system, yes. Why?"

"Where's it housed?"

She frowned. "In the furnace room. It's off a corridor leading from the main part of the house to the kitchens."

I leaned forward, holding up a finger. "This is important. So if you're not one hundred per cent certain, say so. Does the air-conditioning system serve the whole house or only part of it?"

She crossed her knees, swinging an ankle as she thought. "That's easy," she decided. "It's in every room in the big house and the kitchens. That is, everywhere, except the servants' rooms."

"So that would include the ballroom and Marika's suite, of course. The room where you say the safe is?"

"Naturally." She removed the cigarette from her lips so that smoke no longer hindered her view of me.

"Tell me about tomorrow night," I insisted. "How many of the local police are going to be inside the house?"

"None," she said promptly. "Marika wouldn't allow it. And there'll only be two outside in the grounds — one on duty at the lodge, the other on the polo field. That's being turned into a car lot."

I knew that the polo field was a good quarter mile from the house.

"That means there'll be nobody hanging around out front, no cars parked there?"

"None," she repeated. "Cars will arrive and leave guests at the front door, then the chauffeurs will drive to the polo field. If people happen to have no chauffeur, our man will do the parking for them."

I couldn't detect a false note in anything she said. As far as I was concerned she'd passed her credibility test. But there were still a few things that I had to know.

"How many servants will be on duty in the house tomorrow night?"

"Everyone. That's nine people. The butler, two housekeepers and six maids. A marquee has been put up for the chauffeurs. The gardeners will be there helping serve refreshments."

Her cigarette carried an inch of ash. I threw it in the fire and held her wrists in my hands.

"Think hard. Are the ballroom windows ever opened?"

Her answer was immediate. "In this weather?" She mimed a shiver.

"O.K. Now here comes the sixty-four dollar question. Could you make certain that everyone in the house is in the ballroom at a given time?"

"There's no need for that," she said calmly. "They already will be. Marika's opening the ball with Mischka. All the servants and policemen have been summoned to attend. Everyone will be there except the man watching the safe. Nothing will shift him, of course."

"Never mind about him," I told her. "What about outsiders, photographers, musicians?"

She disengaged her hands. "The photographers will be in the ballroom taking pictures and there won't be any musicians. Marika had one of her thrifty spells and got a discotheque to take care of the music. A girl's coming up from Zürich to play the records. Now if you don't tell me what all this is about, Paul, I'm going to scream."

It was the last thing I could imagine her doing. I grinned. I had fed her all the clues and even then she hadn't guessed.

"Gas," I said quietly. "Nerve gas. We've got enough to stop a regiment of soldiers. When everyone's assembled in the ballroom, I leave, locking that one pair of doors. The gas goes into the air ducts. It's completely tasteless and odorless. In a couple of minutes' time two hundred people will be asleep on the floor. They'll wake up three hours later with nothing worse than a hangover."

She raised her hands in silent salute, her expression delighted. "*Wunderbar!* Now you can see why I waited for someone like you. It's brilliant, Paul. You wear a mask, of course. I'm worried about the man upstairs, that's the only thing. The gas might reach him later."

Her grip on things encouraged me. "Somebody'll be there to catch him when he falls," I answered. "And the telephones will be out of order. Who keeps the key to the safe?"

"There are two. The detective on duty has one. The other's always with Marika. She carries it in her handbag."

"No questions?" I probed.

A fresh look of interest showed behind her smile. "Then it's not just Marika's jewelry. It's Grace's and all the others." She named thirty women famed for their collections of gems.

"Right," I said briskly. Even thinking about it exhilarated me. "We'll leave nothing. And don't worry about your share, Uschi. There are still a few things that you don't know about me. One is that when I pledge my word I keep it. You'll get everything that's coming to you."

She made a face and then smiled at me. "I've heard that expression before, you know. I'm not so sure I like it."

"I'll keep my word and so will the others."

She took my jacket by the lapels and pulled my head around till our lips met.

"Don't you think I trust you?" she whispered. "I don't break a promise either."

"Then we know how we stand," I said.

166

She was playing with my lighter, the flame spurting and dwindling. Her face was pensive.

"Only up to a point. I want to know what happens after tomorrow night. After the ball is over."

I remembered the old, old song but made as if I didn't understand.

"Two days from now the money will be in Zürich. You'll be able to draw every penny that's coming to you. Only you wouldn't do that, would you? You're too smart."

She looked up. "I wouldn't do that, no. That isn't what I was thinking about, Paul. Are we going to give ourselves that chance — together?"

I took the lighter away from her, irritated by the way she kept snapping it open and shut.

"Why don't we just take one thing at a time?"

She hugged her knees, staring into the fire, a younger and somehow more vulnerable version of herself.

"That makes me a little bit sad. I don't think there are many men who would give me an answer like that."

The sunshine had gone from the room but the smell of burning leaves persisted. Something told me to tread delicately.

"Maybe not, but you'll be better off with me in the long run."

Her eyes warmed. "Is that a promise, Paul?"

I found her lips with mine. Her fingers stroked the back of my neck. I broke away after a couple of seconds.

"Let's get our feet on the ground," I suggested. "Here's what's going to happen. My friends and I arrive in the Rolls. One of them drives, the other's hidden in the trunk. They drop me at the house, drive around and park in the garage. You'll have left the kitchen door open. The maids will be in the ballroom when the gas is carried in."

She nodded slowly. "Meanwhile the plane is waiting, ready to take off."

My face stiffened with resentment. "Who told you about the plane?"

She burst out laughing. "Don't look so hurt, Paul. I'm a lone woman fending for myself, remember. *Of course* I thought of a plane. I drove out to the airfield this morning. It wasn't difficult to find out that there was just one aircraft under charter — to a Mr. Paul Henderson. Don't worry, darling. It was all done very discreetly. I want you to listen to me. It doesn't take three men to deliver the jewelry to whoever is going to buy it. So you'll stay with me."

The words dropped into my brain like depth charges. "You're suggesting that I'm found in the ballroom!"

Her waving hand dismissed the outrage in my voice. "Why not — just like all the other guests."

"You're out of your mind," I said with determination. "Are you forgetting that I have a record? The police would crucify me!"

She moued prettily. "Nonsense. You're going to be properly invited. I've already mentioned it to Marika. I told her I'd met you in London years ago. She doesn't care. Half the people invited she doesn't know, anyway. Of course the police will question you. They'll question me, too. You told me so yesterday. But what can they do — absolutely nothing. We'll be that much stronger together, Paul. If you're there I'll have more confidence. Not only that — it's what I want."

The note of authority in the last words reminded me of the reality of the situation.

"The others may not go for it," I warned.

Her mouth was contemptuous. "The others! I'm sick of hearing about them. They'll do what they're told. You'll have to hire another car, Paul. The Rolls is much too conspicuous. You want something that the policeman on the gate won't remember. And don't look so glum. I know what I'm doing. When the time comes for questioning, your partners won't be here. You and I will just sit tight and wait for the scandal to subside. Our money will be safely in the bank. Marika's due in Nassau at the beginning of next month. I'll tell her before then."

"Tell her what?" I demanded.

"That I'm leaving to get married."

"To get married!" I said aghast.

She cocked her head on one side. "It's about the only reason that will make sense to her. Don't worry. I won't hold you to it."

I looked at her with disbelief. The fire collapsed in a burst of flame.

"You really mean all this stuff?" I challenged.

She nodded casually. "It's the only way. It's either that or nothing. Talk to your friends. I'm sure they'll understand."

I made one last attempt to shake her. "There's just one thing: Mischka. If I stay he's going to smell a rat."

She reached behind the sofa for her coat and hat. "Leave Mischka to me. Meet me at the Gambrinus tomorrow morning, eleven sharp. We'll go over the final details and I'll bring your invitation card and costume. It's a fancy-dress ball, remember. The skating is off, by the way."

I held her coat as she shrugged into it. My hands itched

to take her by the throat and squeeze till the smile left her lips forever. She turned and kissed me full on the mouth, and I had to stop myself from wiping it away.

"Don't lose your nerve, *Kätzchen*. I won't let anything happen to you."

I prowled around the house for a long time after she had left, like a dog that knows he's been spotted burying a bone. I shifted the gas canisters and my burglar's kit to the garage. An inspection pit covered with dirty piled planks made a perfect hiding place. I was still uneasy, as though an eye was watching me through a peephole. I wandered upstairs to Chalice's bedroom. I opened the right-hand drawer in the highboy between the two beds. Crying Eddie's socks were neatly rolled, the pile of freshly laundered handkerchiefs crisp with a touch of starch. I felt beneath and found a stack of bills, Swiss francs and dollars. There was something else there too — a picture of a handsome-looking woman at some Cockney junket. A coach was drawn up in the background. Men wearing paper hats were holding up beer bottles. It had to be Eddie's mother. She glared into the lens as if her drunken husband were holding the camera. Eddie had evidently taken his passport with him. The other drawer held nothing but a box of cheroots and some paperbacks dealing with guerrilla warfare. I'd have to look further afield.

What I wanted was in a shoe bag at the bottom of the clothes closet. The two guns inside were stubby-nosed Belgian automatics of .38 caliber. Both clips were fully charged and a shell was pumped into each breech. I wiped off the guns with my handkerchief and put them back in the shoe bag. I'd guessed that my partners were carrying guns, but I'd never asked nor had they volunteered. It was a relief to be sure about something.

I went down to the drawing room again. It was already dark outside. The only light came from the fire. Six had come and gone when head lamps swept the front of the house. Seconds later I heard the Rolls being maneuvered into the garage. I opened the door and caught Sophie in my arms. Her face was icy and there was chocolate around her mouth. The words tumbled out excitedly.

"We went much higher than the mountains, Papa. Higher, 'n higher, 'n higher!"

Chalice came into the room grinning. "She's right, mate. That was really something. That Baxter's quite a driver. Six countries we seen since we left!"

Sophie kicked her way to the ground. "I'm hungry."

I looked down at her. "Take your things off and wash and I'll fix you something."

Chalice threw his bowler at the sofa. It was getting more dilapidated by the day.

"That plane shifts along, Paul. I worked it out that we'll be in Antwerp in an hour and a half."

"Brussels," I corrected, "not Antwerp. They're eighteen miles apart and we've got to break the chain. I'll arrange for a car to be waiting."

The door opened. Crying Eddie lounged over and warmed his hands at the fire. We nodded at one another shortly. We'd maintained a guarded civility since the flare-up the previous night. I continued:

"We're going to send Baxter back to Rome to pick up a Mr. Leonard who won't show, obviously. We'll give Baxter time to sleep and refuel then bring him back to London. That should do it."

Chalice's bloodhound eyes searched my face. "O.K., mate, what is it? I can smell something up your sleeve."

I wriggled my shoulders. "It's the Baroness's idea, not mine. You two are taking the gear to Van der Pouk. Sophie and I are staying."

They glanced at one another sharply before looking back at me. "She's crazy," Eddie said shortly.

I made a gesture of denial. "Like a fox. She's making sure that she gets her end. Sophie and I are being held as hostages." I explained Uschi's revamped plan in detail.

Chalice moved to his favorite spot in front of the fireplace, scratching his back luxuriously against the mantel.

"You mean you're really going through with this?"

I spread my hands. "What else is there to do? She's no fool and she certainly means business. The alternative is to get our things together and blow town tonight. You know how I feel about that." Something stopped me from telling them about Uschi's plan for our joint future.

He turned around, put his arms on the mantel, and leaned into them, brooding. After a while he swung back to face me.

"I ain't going to tell you what to do, mate. It's up to you. All I'm saying is that she just might have got something. Look at it this way. Me and Ed is never seen near the premises, not so we'll be remembered, anyway. By the time those slags are picking themselves off the ballroom floor, we'll be five hundred miles away. What can the law do? Your passport's clean, you've been properly invited. Sweet fuck all, that's what they can do. I wouldn't say it's my idea of passing a pleasant weekend, but it's worth thinking about at least. We can have the best lawyer in the country up here holding your hand."

Nerves prompted a yawn. "I'm meeting her at eleven tomorrow morning to go over things for the last time in detail."

"What time does the ball start?" Chalice demanded.

Sophie arrived just in time to hear the final words. "I want to go, Papa. Please, Papa, may I go to the ball?"

"You may not," I said firmly. "And don't whine. A fancy-dress ball isn't for small girls."

She searched her mind for the most cutting rejoinder. "I'm going to marry Eddie," she announced.

My prospective son-in-law showed well-cared-for teeth. "And don't get no funny ideas about coming to live with us, neither."

I took Sophie to the kitchen, sat her on a barstool and broke eggs for scrambling. A pair of candlesticks stood on the draining board. She started breaking off pieces of wax and dropping them into the waste-disposal unit. It had been a long, hard day and I guess my voice betrayed it.

"Let's knock it off, sweetheart. Just for five minutes."

She stopped immediately, turning her blue serious eyes on me. "I won't marry him if you don't want me to, Papa."

It was all there in the warmth of her small body — hope, happiness, everything that was left in my life that was good. Only loving her wasn't enough. She was a female in a man's world. The time would come when she'd be beyond my reach and alone. When that happened, she had to have a real chance. And I was only hours away from being able to give it to her. Chalice's head peered around the door.

"Skomielna's just been in. He says he wants to see you, urgent."

I tucked a napkin around Sophie's neck and spooned the scrambled egg onto a plate.

"As soon as you're through eating, go take a bath. I won't be long."

Skomielna answered my knock as if he had been waiting for it. He was wearing red velvet pants and an orange cashmere sweater. He shut the door, shivering, and wrapped an arm around my neck.

"Paul, my dear fellow."

His arm gave me a feeling of claustrophobia and I shook it off impatiently.

"What was it you wanted to see me about?"

The room was a smaller replica of the drawing room across the way. An aromatic curl of smoke drifted up from a bowl on the low table between the brocade armchairs. He poured two glasses of sherry and handed me one. It was obviously not his first. Looking at his stretched face and masklike smile, I wondered how he kept it up at his age. He cocked his head on one side.

"Did you enjoy your afternoon?"

I held the glass halfway between the chair rest and my mouth. A trick of light turned him into a macaw parrot.

"Oh, dear," he squawked. "We *are* touchy tonight, aren't we! Would you allow me to give you some advice, Paul?"

I sipped at the sherry cautiously. "That depends on what area it covers."

"Youth," he said, like some ancient coquette being asked to remember a bygone lover. "I'm worried about you, dear boy. Very worried."

Experience has taught that when people say this it's themselves they're usually worried about.

"Is your worry of a general or a specific character?" I asked.

He closed his eyes as though wounded. He seemed to mock himself so often that it was hard to know whether or not he was putting me on.

174

"Your direct approach is quite refreshing," he said, opening his eyes again. "But I fear it may contribute to your downfall. You've been to bed with Uschi, of course."

"I think you're getting a wee bit out of line," I suggested.

He backed off a couple of steps, refusing the suggestion with outstretched hands.

"Come on, now!" he coaxed. "These Anglo-Saxon attitudes are ridiculous. I'm concerned with *you*, not the lady's reputation. Don't you understand that?"

"Not too well," I said frankly. "Give me a clue."

He pirouetted, looking at himself in the mirror. "I'm an old trollop, dear boy. A greedy, curious old transvestite. Scandal's like snuff to me. I breathe it in with gratitude. I find it strange that of all people Uschi should have been playing the whore in my house."

I kept my temper. My voice was quiet. "You're an old man but you seem to like living dangerously."

He wrung his answer from clasped hands dramatically. "I'll admit it. Go ahead and beat me up — it's no more than I deserve."

I wouldn't have touched the old rogue and he knew it. Nor could I leave. I had to hear him out.

"What exactly is it you have to say?" I asked him.

He wagged his head. "His Imperial Majesty once asked the same question of a great-uncle of mine. I can do no better than to quote my uncle's reply: 'Permit me to relate an anecdote, sire.' An hour ago I was in the village buying petrol. I do this at the same place always — the BP station near the lake. There's a young man who works there — but that's another story. The street is very narrow at this point, with no room for the pumps which are up on the sixth floor. One drives up a ramp. There were several cars in front of me and

I had to wait my turn. I was sitting there, idly enough, looking down at the street. I don't know if you've seen the place but there's a photographer's shop there, on the opposite side of the road to the pumps. It's almost on the corner of Seestrasse. Do you know where I mean?"

I knew where he meant well enough. Seestrasse was the shortest way to reach the lake from the ice stadium.

"I know," I said.

He inspected an eyebrow in the mirror before continuing. "I want you to listen very carefully. There's an apartment above the photographer's shop with three windows. One must be the bathroom, the others some sort of living room. The curtains were not drawn at the time I'm speaking about. I can understand why. There's nothing opposite except the back wall of the post office. I happened to be in a privileged position — if 'privileged' is the right choice of word. Anyway, a man suddenly came into view. Big, blond and obviously German. He was stark naked. The lights were out in the apartment, but my eyes are still dependable. I'll admit that in the next seconds I started to doubt them. Who should come into the man's arms but Uschi. She was naked, too."

I can remember walking in downtown Toronto and seeing a man on the sidewalk in front of me suddenly disappear down an open chute. I had the same sense of incredulity now as then.

"You don't expect me to believe that, do you?" I asked.

There was a brilliance in his eyes that was the combination of liquor and malice.

"Of course you believe it, dear boy. It's too easy to corroborate anyway. She must have gone straight from you to him."

176

A dozen implications crowded my mind, but I gave him what was meant to be a casual smile.

"They come and they go, Mischka. I'm too long in the tooth to get involved anymore."

He replenished his glass, chattering away with his back turned to me.

"That's what I thought. Nevertheless the lady's behavior merits a sharp lesson. We don't want you to miss the festivities but afterward, perhaps . . . I could probably help you think of something. Nothing like a queer for a bitchy revenge, you know." He smiled like an alligator.

I came to my feet. "I'm grateful for your interest, Mischka, but I didn't get in that deep. Thanks all the same."

He waved his glass. "Don't be too kind to her, Paul. She doesn't deserve it."

I had an impression that he'd be delighted to assist at her downfall — that he might even be gunning for her job.

"Good night," I said. "And don't bother getting up." I hurried over to the big house. It was freezing hard under a sky that hid the moon and stars. Chalice turned his head as the door opened. He was lying on the sofa with his shoes off.

"I been thinking what we're going to do about the buyer, mate. Didn't you say he won't deal with strangers?"

I shifted his legs and sat down on the sofa beside him. "It doesn't look as if he'll have to, Harry. Listen to this one." I gave him Skomielna's story word for word.

His hand came up in a commanding gesture. "Wait a minute, mate! How do we know he's not trying to mix it? These old fags spend their lives making trouble. I've seen it — Doll's club is full of them."

I wasn't one person beyond all doubt about the subject.

"No, Harry. You were right the first time. We've been framed."

He started pulling his shoes on, grunting with effort. "You know where this apartment is, do you?"

"Right behind the post office," I explained. "It'll take us fifteen minutes to get there on foot."

He stood up. "Then what are we waiting for? Get your gear. I'll tell Eddie where we're going. He can stay and watch the baby."

I retrieved my skeleton keys, stuck a pencil flashlight in my pocket, and collected my overcoat. We walked downtown without speaking, each of us busy with his own problems. Seestrasse ran parallel with the southern lake shore. An illuminated sign located the garage. There was a repair shop at street level. A ramp climbed up to the sixth floor. Anyone looking down from it would have an uninterrupted view of the photography store fifty yards away, and an even better view of the apartment above. We were only a block away from the bustle of Bahnhofstrasse but it was quiet. The only light except that from the streetlamps came from the garage, the photographer's display, and an inn that overlooked the lake. We strolled up the street and affected an interest in the Japanese cameras. It was bitterly cold. Chalice's leathery face had acquired an undertone of blue on our journey down. He had pulled his bowler hat down low on his ears and looked part of some third-rate vaudeville act. The post-office yard behind us was protected by a high brick wall. I glanced up at the windows overhead. The curtains weren't drawn. The entrance to the apartment was no more than six feet away. The only lock on the door was a simple-looking mortise. I pulled the key ring out of my pocket.

"Cover me."

The first three keys were no good. The fourth — a dropped-E pattern — turned the lock off. I motioned Chalice into the small hallway in front of me. A carpeted flight of stairs faced us. There wasn't a sound in the place.

"Stay here," I whispered. "If anyone comes through that door, jump him. Whatever you do, make sure he doesn't get a chance to yell."

Chalice stationed himself behind the door. I smelled Uschi's scent when I was halfway up the stairs. The studio apartment above had a living room, kitchen, and bath. There were rugs on the waxed parquet floor, a couple of German rocking chairs, and the walls were painted white. A silk spread depicting peacocks covered the bed. The paintings and bric-a-brac gave me the impression that the apartment belonged to a woman. I peered out the back windows. The stillness of the lake below was unnatural after the activity of the day. Pounded snow marked the tracks where the horses had raced earlier. The lights from the Palace Hotel illuminated the scene, the grandstands standing ghostly gray on the perimeter.

I snapped on the flashlight and put it between my teeth, leaving my hands free. The first room I explored was the bathroom. A drip-dry sweater was hanging over the tub. There was a razor and a bottle of Calèche on the shelf under the mirror. Inside the small drawer was a plastic dispenser half filled with birth-control pills. I went back to the living room. I wasted no time with the locked cupboard, but went directly to the desk. I struck oil first time. There was a German passport on top of a wallet. It identified the owner as Horst-Helmut Pfeiffer, born in Altona, 19 March, 1940. His occupation was given as computer programmer. Skomielna's description was accurate enough. The photograph showed a blond-haired man with a hard jaw and combative eyes. There were five page of visas, most of them for South American countries. The exit and entrance stamps covered most of Europe. Pfeiffer was a much-traveled man. I opened the wallet. There was nothing inside it but a couple of snapshots and some faded medal ribbons. The top picture was of a Luftwaffe pilot standing beside a Messerschmidt. There was a strong resemblance to Pfeiffer about the man's face. The other picture was in color and had been taken with a good camera. It featured Uschi standing in a forest clearing, holding a leashed Dalmation. She was tanned and smiling as I'd never seen her smile. The inscription on the back of the snapshot left nothing to the imagination:

For my husband before God, my lover and comrade,
forever your Uschi

I put the wallet and passport back in their original places. The right-hand drawer contained a P-38 fitted with a silencer. The clip was full and there was a spare box of shells. Underneath the phone was a folded piece of paper. The message was written in German.

7:20 P.M. I came back to tell you to be sure to watch her on television tonight, 9:30. I'll be here tomorrow afternoon, two o'clock sharp. No problems, darling. Love you,

USCHI

I memorized the phone number and ran back down the stairs. Chalice already had the street door open. We backed out, raising our hats as though saying farewell to our host. There was nobody in sight to appreciate the act. Chalice fell into step with me.

"Bad?"

"I'll tell you later," I said. "Let's go across to the inn."

His face was still blue with cold and he looked ridiculous in the bowler, but I was glad to have him by my side. The timber-and-plaster building bulged with age. There were painted balconies up on the second story and an enormous sign depicting a golden swan. We pushed past a heavy leather curtain into a crowded drinking hall. There were too many closely packed bodies, too much cigar smoke and garlic sausage. A guy was picking on a zither, the audience banging out time with the bottoms of their tankards. There were no seats free. We found a space against the wall and ordered a couple of beers from a damp-haired waitress in a dirndl. She pointed to a door when I asked for the proprietor.

"I'll be right back," I said to Chalice. The inner room was equally smoky but considerably quieter. A bull-necked man wearing a collarless gray flannel shirt was leaning on the small bar watching two old men in knickerbockers play dominoes. All three favored me with a brief hostile stare reserved for strangers. I countered with a smile.

"Schnapps, please!"

The man behind the bar hitched up his sleeves. They were fastened with elastic bands. He moved like some prehistoric monster staking out his territory.

"Are you the owner of the inn?" I asked.

He shoved a small glass of colorless liquid over at me. "Schnapps!"

I emptied the glass blindly and stepped back feeling as if I'd been scalped. I wiped my eyes spluttering.

He leaned his forearms on the bar. "I am the owner, yes."

"Give me another drink," I said bravely, "and have one

yourself." He served them with glasses of water as chasers. The interview was obviously closed as far as he was concerned, but I stayed right where I was.

"I'm looking for accommodation. Do you happen to have anything free?"

He was smoking an Italian stogie, a crooked black affair with a plastic mouthpiece. He took it from between nicotine-stained teeth, spitting at the stove carefully before answering.

"In April 1973."

The old men at the table must have heard the crack many times before, but one of them slapped his knee so hard I thought he had done himself an injury. The heat from the porcelain stove was oppressive.

"It was for a friend," I said doggedly, wiping my face and neck. "He doesn't care how much he pays."

The landlord cleared a space in the smoke screen between us and aimed his answer through it.

"There are lots of people who don't mind what they pay."

I kept after him. "I heard that the apartment over the photography store is for rent. Do you happen to know if that's true?"

He shook his head shortly. "Not true."

I scratched the back of my neck, looking dubious. "That's odd. The man who told me seemed to know what he was talking about."

The landlord's face darkened. "And I know what I'm talking about — I should do; my daughter takes care of the apartment. Fraulein Seiler's place is rented for the season. There are no rooms in Todtsee, mister. No houses, no apartments. Try Gstaad or St. Moritz." He spat the names out as if they left a bad taste in his mouth.

I pried Chalice loose from the wall and we went outside. My lungs gulped the cold air gratefully. We were almost out of the courtyard when a red Triumph shot by and drew up outside Pfeiffer's apartment. Pfeiffer climbed from behind the wheel and went inside. Lights came on upstairs. He was down again after a couple of minutes, this time wearing a black astrakhan hat and a coat with a fur collar. He was even bigger than I thought and meaner looking. We watched the tail lamps move to the end of the street and out of sight. I touched Chalice's arm.

"Let's go. His name's Pfeiffer, he's a German. There's no doubt that he's shacking up with the Baroness and he's got a P-38 up there fitted with a silencer."

Chalice slipped, almost going down on the icy sidewalk. He grabbed at me to right himself.

"That sounds real cosy. What else do we know about him?"

"He's a computer programmer who spends a lot of his time traveling. I guess he doesn't like noise, hence the silencer."

We were climbing the long slope toward the banked curves of the bob run. We went the last couple of hundred yards in complete silence.

"Are you thinking what I'm thinking?" I asked quietly.

Chalice stopped, holding his hand to his side till he caught his breath. "I don't know, mate. But I probably am."

Eddie was waiting for us in the kitchen, sipping a glass of milk and wearing a camel's-hair robe over yellow silk pajamas. I left Chalice to straighten him out and took a look at Sophie. She was breathing heavily, her arms around the rubber doll. I sat down, trying to think calmly. I started with the fact that Uschi and Pfeiffer were lovers. Whichever way I went from there it came out the same in the end. They were more than lovers. They were confederates in a scheme that had a dual purpose. The first part called for us to commit the robbery. The second would be designed to trim us of the proceeds. What we had to know was *how*. If ever I felt as though I needed moral support it was now. It helped somehow that Chalice had gone to the apartment with me. He accepted things as they were without apportioning blame. It was Eddie I was worried about. He was lying in his chair rather than sitting in it, his shoulder blades where his rump should have been. He barely lifted his head to look at me.

"O.K., everybody quiet," said Chalice holding his hand in the air. "I'm trying to think." He took a turn to the wall and back, five good steps each way, the precise length of a cell in a military prison. Then he anchored himself on the end of the sofa.

"Suppose we was the law and we sussed the Baroness and her boy friend. Say we knew they was up to something only we didn't have no evidence against them. What would we do?"

Crying Eddie hauled himself erect. "That's easy. We'd take them in and produce a statement where they said something like 'No, Officer, I never was in Blumenthal's premises in my life. I wasn't coming out of no back window having left my pal Paddy Murphy 'round the corner with the car.'"

Chalice's face was sour. "O.K., you can take your clown's hat off and go back to sleep. How about you, Paul?"

I gave it a little thought. "Put a tail on them, tap their phones, maybe. That kind of thing."

Crying Eddie shut his eyes ostentatiously and chewed a

match. Chalice nodded.

"We ain't got that sort of time, have we? One thing's obvious: the Baroness is out to screw us and Pfeiffer's part of the act. Do you agree?"

Crying Eddie applauded, his eyes still shut. "Call me when the dancing girls come on."

"As far as we know," Chalice continued, "they don't meet in public — they wouldn't want to, would they — so whatever they have to say to one another is said in that apartment. Are you with me?"

Crying Eddie groaned sepulchrally. "If he ain't I am. Here we go with the little black box again. I'll lay odds on it."

Chalice left the room without giving his partner the benefit of a reply. He came back, carrying a small plastic container.

He sat down, tapping the case with a forefinger. "This is a tape recorder but with a difference. There are no wires, just the mike and this." He opened the case and produced a device that would have fitted into a large can of beans. He followed it with a metal disc the size of a silver dollar and maybe four times as thick. "The mike. It's got a suction cap and it's magnetic. Plant that and you can sit in your car a mile away and hear what's being said."

"You're being modest, mate," Crying said ironically.

"Don't pay him no heed," answered Chalice. "This little beauty has earned us some fair money on two occasions and it's kept him out of the pokey at least once. We're going to bug Pfeiffer's apartment." He put the mike and speaker back in the case.

I shifted in my seat. "There's not much time left for that either."

185

"Enough," he said. "We're not going to make another move until we're certain what their plan is. How long do you think it would take you to get into the place a second time, Paul?"

"Seconds," I answered promptly. "I know which key to use now. It's running things fine, but morning would be best if we're going to do it. He's not likely to stay around while the place is being cleaned."

His expression was dubious. "I'd say lure Pfeiffer out but we can't afford to have him suspect anything. That's our strength now, keeping everything up our sleeve. What time are you seeing her tomorrow morning?"

"Eleven — downtown."

"Then if we haven't gone in by then, you can leave the key with me and Eddie," he said.

Crying stretched his legs. "I got a much better plan. We simply grab the geezer and make sure he's out of circulation. Then we do what we was going to do in the first place."

"That's brilliant!" Chalice's voice was charged with sarcasm. "That's strategy, that is. And what does she do when she finds out he's missing, may I ask?"

Crying Eddie took the match from between his teeth. "We grab her, too."

"You got grab on the brain," Chalice said witheringly. "You ought to be in Brazil or somewhere with them revolutionaries. Simmer down, mate. Let your brain cool off."

I looked at the clock and landed on my feet. "The box — she's on at nine-thirty!"

Sophie woke up as we came into the room. I switched on the set and sat down, holding her hand. The camera discovered a young man with an economic haircut and fulsome smile standing in the middle of the ballroom at Shahpur.

186

The camera panned slowly, lingering on the gilt, plush, and velvet furnishings, the cascade of glass falling from the ceiling, then back to the interviewer in close-up. He gave us the breathtaking news with buttery reverence.

"And now, ladies and gentlemen, the Swiss television network has the privilege of introducing you to the hostess of this magnificent mansion — the lady whose twinkling feet and delicate beauty have endeared her to millions of people the world over. Ladies and gentlemen, *Marika Bergen!*"

She was dressed in some sort of a national costume with a full skirt and laced-up bodice. The make-up squad had done a good job on her, creating softness where there was none, disguising the wrinkles of greed and petulance. Her German had a strong singsong accent.

"Thank you, Herr Fischli. Good evening, ladies and gentlemen. I always think of Switzerland as my second home. My only regret is that all of you cannot be here tomorrow night to join in the festivities."

She touched her fingers to her throat, refracted light from the diamonds flashing into the lens. The camera retreated slowly till it showed her at full length. An unidentified arm offered a bouquet of long-stemmed roses, and she dropped a curtsy. I turned the set off and covered Sophie. She hadn't spoken throughout the whole thing.

I followed them upstairs, yawning. Chalice stopped outside his door.

"Who's going to take care of the baby tomorrow?"

Crying Eddie was emptying drawers already, his bag on top of the bed.

"The school runs a bus service," I said. "I'll call and have them pick her up."

"O.K.," he said. "Sleep sound."

It was a long time before I even came near the edge of it. When I did, my last conscious memory was of tumbling into a bottomless pit with Pfeiffer leaning after me, smiling.

Chapter Six

THE UNTOUCHED GLASS of water came into focus, the clothes strewn over the floor. There was a strange hush throughout the house. I scrambled up in bed. The window ledge was fat with two inches of new snow. The flakes that were still falling evoked memories of Ontario winters — of blocked highways and marooned cars, villages and towns isolated by blizzards. I swung out of bed and took the phone. There was nobody on duty at the Swissair desk. The switchboard operator put me through to the control tower. A bored voice answered my inquiry. The guy sounded as if he had answered the same question too many times that morning. Scheduled flights were taking off according to program. The runways were clear and better weather was expected by ten o'clock. It wasn't eight yet. By the time I'd finished showering, his point had been proven. The gray snow clouds were breaking up and the fall had almost stopped.

I hurried down to the kitchen. Sophie was wearing her yellow sweater and her ski pants. She chopped the top from a boiled egg and offered it to me. I pushed it away, shuddering, and poured myself a strong cup of tea.

"Have you looked outside?" said Chalice. Neither of them

was in uniform. Chalice was wearing a herringbone tweed, Crying Eddie a doeskin suit.

"I just called the airport," I said. "Traffic's normal."

"I dreamt I went to the ball," Sophie announced.

"And that's as near as you'll ever get to it," I replied. "You're going to the playground again. Here's ten francs to buy rides." The other two reached into their pockets mechanically. Sophie collected their offerings. Breakfast deteriorated into a silent affair with nobody saying much beyond "pass the salt." The bus came for Sophie at a quarter to nine. I tipped the man heavily, and he promised to have her back by four that afternoon. We piled the dishes in the sink and went up to Chalice's bedroom. The maid was due at any minute. Chalice turned the key in the door and pulled the two guns out of a drawer. He gave one to Crying and sighted down the barrel of the other with an air of expert familiarity. Their bags were packed and their beds neatly made. They must have been up very early. I sat down facing them. Chalice put his gun in his jacket pocket. His partner followed suit.

"Now," said Chalice comfortably. "We been making bleedin' mistakes. We can't afford no more."

"It's a big forest," I said. "You're bound to bang into trees."

Crying was buffing his nails. He suspended the operation. "That's a deep statement if ever I heard one."

Chalice gave me the case with the recorder. He watched as I twisted the mike, activating it. His dark eyes were approving.

"That's it. The tape'll run for an hour."

My stomach was complaining windily. It was the waiting

that always killed me. The other two had eaten like truck drivers, cereal, ham and eggs, a dozen pieces of toast at least.

"What are we doing about the car?" I asked.

"Nothing." Chalice's heavy shoulders dismissed the subject. "Leave it here and put it down to expenses. Split three ways it don't come to much."

No one was thinking in terms of running anymore. It was as if the latest developments had hardened our resolution.

"That's out," I said, shaking my head. "Nobody abandons a six-thousand-pound automobile without having good reason. It would be normal enough to ship it back to England. Why not just do that?"

"Do it then," Chalice said carelessly. "It's registered in your name, remember. What are you going to say to this bird when you meet her?"

I leaned back, looking out through the window. The garden was unfamiliar under its fresh blanket of snow. I'd been asking myself the same question ever since we left Pfeiffer's apartment.

"I'll take up where I left off yesterday," I answered. "As if I didn't know a thing."

He was watching a spot on the carpet between his feet. "Once you're in that house tonight, she ain't going to let you out of her sight, you realize that, don't you?"

"I know what she *thinks* she's going to do," I corrected. "I left her with the impression that there's only one gas mask between us. I'll have it in the ballroom with me."

Eddie removed the match he was chewing. "I wish I knew what those bastards are up to. It worries me them knowing and we don't."

"We'll know soon enough," said Chalice. "She ain't going

to Pfeiffer's apartment this afternoon to tell him she loves him. They'll be talking things over, just like us."

Chalice brooded. Crying Eddie whistled for a moment and then broke off.

"Another thing: what about Old Bill when he comes around my house asking, 'What was you doing in Switzerland?' and so on. What do I tell him?"

I lit the second cigarette of the day and took a deep drag. "You remember the golden rule — no prosecution without evidence. The first thing they'll be looking for is any sign of sudden wealth. With you two it doesn't matter so much. But I'll be back in that dump of mine in Chelsea, waiting for them. Let them suspect what they like. Being in Todtsee's no crime. Uschi won't open her mouth too wide, remember. She'd have to explain why she invited me to the ball in the first place. My feeling is that the law will stay on our tails for a bit, hoping to be led to the loot. When that doesn't happen, the heat'll die down."

"That's right," Chalice put in. "It ain't going to be the Yard's headache. What happens here in Switzerland. If they do come tapping on our doors, it'll be because Interpol asks them to. Maybe it'll be the Heavy Mob with search warrants. Maybe it'll be a copper from the local station. There's no way of telling."

"That's what I wanted to say," I answered. "You two are in the clear but with me they can produce certain facts. I *did* charter an airplane — I *did* hire this house — I *was* invited to the ball. My point is that I could have done all that with larceny in my heart at the beginning. But when I ran into Greasy George I got scared and called the whole thing off. Someone else must have made the hit."

Chalice's forehead creased. "I don't go for that, mate. Why say you had larceny in your heart in the first place?"

I leaned forward, making my point. "You're getting me wrong. I'm not talking about saying all this to the law. All I want to do is leak a couple of things that will put the idea into their minds."

Chalice's face was graphic. "I still don't like it, mate. You do what you like but if them ponces come around wanting to talk to me, they'll only do it in the presence of a mouthpiece. Them passports will be burned the moment we're through customs. I'll make them prove that we even left England."

I let it drop. "Then that's the way I'll play it, Harry. With a couple of hundred thousand apiece who cares about details!"

We talked on for another half an hour, going over the basic aspects of our plan. No matter what Uschi and her boy friend had in mind, the elements remained constant. It was Eddie who remembered that the gas would have the effect of relaxing muscles, that the jewelry would come off that much easier. We worked it out that the average haul would go around eight ounces, which meant fifty pounds in the aggregate. Any one of us could carry that amount without looking lopsided. We made up our minds that the best bet would be to buy one of those magnesium-framed cases with a steel-core handle. The metal is covered with leather in a classy production unlikely to fall apart at an inopportune moment.

"O.K.," said Chalice. "It's nine-twenty — time to make a move."

The drapes were still drawn tight in Skomielna's quarters.

He'd left the Porsche parked in the usual slapdash fashion. The roof and windshield were covered with snow. There was no one around to see us leave in the Rolls. Seestrasse had an entirely different aspect in daylight. The sun had broken through and the sky had lifted. A double horse box was parked on the lake shore. Two rugged-up thoroughbreds were cantering around the track, powdered snow flying behind them. Their goggled jockeys were high on the animals' necks, clinging there like monkeys. We came into the street from the west and drove up the ramp to the gas pumps. It wasn't ten yet but there was a line of cars waiting at the washing bays. We left the Rolls with an overalled receptionist and went into the waiting room. I stationed myself at the window, turning the pages of a magazine. The windows of the Pfeiffer apartment were reflecting sunshine, making it impossible to see in. Another quarter-hour and a woman hurried across the street, coming from the inn. She cleaned her feet carefully on the scraper outside the apartment and let herself in with a key. I motioned to Crying.

"On your toes, Eddie."

He lounged outside, professing an interest in the cars being washed. Five minutes afterward Pfeiffer emerged wearing a dark-blue duffle coat with the hood over his head. By the time he'd reached the garage, Eddie was halfway down the ramp. His pickup was no more than a neat side-step out onto the street that brought him twenty yards behind the German. Chalice and I watched the pair as far as the lake. Another horse box was being unloaded, the animal rearing and plunging dangerously. Pfeiffer joined the group of onlookers. I saw Eddie's head on the edge of the crowd. I went outside and exchanged two coins for cartons of coffee from the vending machine. We drank them standing, looking down into the street. Half an hour afterward the woman reappeared. She dumped some garbage in a can outside the front door and hurried back to the inn. Chalice went after her. We'd arranged that if she showed signs of returning, he would throw a block. Eddie would stick close to Pfeiffer and use the same tactics if necessary.

Breaking into a house in daytime requires no more than the right tool and plenty of self-assurance. I used the skeleton key with the air of a man entering his own house. One turn of the wrist and I was in. The studio smelled of floor polish and air freshener. Everything was spotless. I looked around for a place to put the mike. The small disc suddenly looked enormous. Chalice had warned me against certain hiding places — the curtains, for instance — the device was too easily dislodged by a casual tug. The water pipes and radiators were out because of vibrations. I crossed the room. Uschi's note had gone from under the phone. I opened up the desk. The P-38 was still in the drawer; Pfeiffer's wallet and passport were there together with a travel agent's folder. The airplane tickets inside had been issued in Hamburg: two first-class singles from Paris to Sao Paulo, Brazil, with an open date. The tickets had been bought in the names of Gunther Wagner and Anneliese Stoll. I put them back in the folder. The heavy oak desk had sunk deep into the carpet and its underfelt. The base of the bottom drawer was no more than a couple of inches from the ground. I pressed the mike firmly against the wood. The suction cap held it, resisting anything but a really determined tug. I straightened up, wiping my gloved hands and looking around. Everything seemed to be in place. I opened a crack in the street door, biding my time for the moment to duck out. Chalice was waiting in the *Trinkhalle* in an aura of stale tobacco smoke and beer. He came over to the door, buttoning his coat. We moved out to the yard and drifted behind a parked car. A pair of oxen were stabled there, hock deep in straw. They suspended their chewing to investigate us, sprays of alfalfa dangling from their mouths. Their breath came sweet and cloying.

"Everything all right, mate?" Chalice inquired.

I told him where I'd planted the mike and about the two airplane tickets. The news didn't seem to please him too much. His expression changed.

"Brazil! We'll have to watch these bastards, Paul. They don't sound like no amateurs to me."

"I want you to pick up Eddie," I said, catching him by the arm. "Tell him to forget about Pfeiffer and keep out of sight. Lose yourselves somewhere. I'll meet you at the garage at half after one."

Clods of frozen snow were scattered over the cobblestones. He booted one into the corner of the yard.

"Look, don't mind me saying this, but watch yourself with the Baroness. Take it nice and easy, like you said. Make sure you don't let her know that we're on to them."

My ears were stinging. I pulled the beaver hat lower. "Don't worry about it, Harry. She's come as far as she's going with me."

Everything I had to do could be done within a radius of a hundred yards. The Gambrinus was obliquely across from the post office. There was a shipping agent in the bank building next door. I walked up to a glass door with a painted sign that read WITWE ROHRER SPEDITION. I pushed the door

open. The girl reached for a pad of printed forms even before I'd finished telling her what I wanted. She made it all
too easy. The Rolls would be collected from the garage. All
I had to do was leave the keys and documents with it. Delivery would be made in care of the Automobile Association,
Port of Dover. I gathered that it would have been all the
same to her if I'd wanted to ship a pair of camels and a belly
dancer. The only thing necessary was to keep peeling off
those thousand-franc bills.

I made two calls from the post office. The first sounded as
if I'd caught Baxter in the middle of eating.

"We're definitely leaving tonight," I announced. "There'll
be three people and a child — that's right, the ones you saw
yesterday. Make all necessary arrangements and be ready to
take off between ten-fifteen and ten-thirty."

"Will do," he said through the last of his cheese sandwich
or whatever it was. "Take off for where, Mr. Henderson?"

"I'm not a hundred per cent sure," I hedged. "I'm waiting
for a phone call."

He cleared his throat, speaking in the manner of one who
deals with an ignoramus who wouldn't know a barometric
digit reading from a hamburger.

"As long as you tell me later, sir. Otherwise there might
be a delay when it comes to clearing. You see, I have to file a
flight plan. The authorities want to know a number of things,
the names of the passengers, for instance, what payload we'll
be carrying. And our destination."

"Make that Paris." I gave him everyone's full name.
"There'll be just us and our hand baggage."

I cradled the receiver. There was no law against a man
changing his mind once he was airborne. I picked up the

phone again and dialed the Antwerp number. There was the usual wait until Van der Pouk's guttural French rumbled in my ear.

"It's Paul," I said quickly. "Now listen. It's tonight. I want a hired car waiting at Brussels Airport from ten o'clock on. I'll be drawing on you heavily, Louis. Do you understand what I mean?"

"I understand," he answered. "All that will be taken care of. You're sure you'll be able to find your way?"

I'd found it often enough before, swathed in yellow oilskins and crouching at the bottom of an open speedboat that bounced from wave to wave, hitting low water with a sickening smack. Van der Pouk conducted his business on the high sea, his yacht well outside territorial waters.

I paid for the calls and went outside. Cars were double parked the whole length of Bahnhofstrasse. It was ten to eleven by the clock over the post-office steps. The sun had gathered heat and the ski lifts were busy on the slopes. A haggard-faced woman with eyes like charcoal smears stood below me on the sidewalk talking to a man in white fur. Any jewel thief worthy of the name would have recognized Arlette Shashoua — the legendary Arlette, millionairess and totally deaf. She lip-read so well that many were ignorant of her secret. She owned four asphalt lakes in Trinidad and the famous twenty-four carat diamond. In spite of her disability no one had ever been able to steal it. It flashed now as she touched the back of her auburn hair. In just a few hours the ring would be ours.

I went down the steps intending to cross over to the Gambrinus. As I stepped off the curb, someone bleeped a horn at me. I turned around, searching both sides of the street.

198

The horn sounded again. I traced the noise to a car fifteen yards away. Uschi was leaning out of the window, beckoning. I climbed in beside her.

"I thought you said the Gambrinus. I was just on my way there."

"This is better," she said. "There are too many people about."

Her coat was bundled on the back seat next to a cardboard box. She was wearing a camel's-hair tam-o'-shanter and matching sweater. Her boots were made with the shaggy fur outside. She smiled at me.

"Take your eyes off Arlette Shashoua, darling. You'll see enough of her tonight. Did you do what I told you to do about the Rolls?"

There was a pack of cigarettes on top of the dash — a brand I'd never seen her use. I was sure that it belonged to Pfeiffer, that he'd sat in this very seat discussing how to deal with me. I took one of the butts and flipped the spent match through the open window.

"I'm getting a hired car this afternoon. By the way, I talked things over with the others and they're willing to go along. There's just one thing. They think I ought to have a lawyer to look after my interests."

"A lawyer!" She touched her fingers to my cheek. "You don't need a lawyer. Mama loves you too much to let anything happen to you."

I smiled until my face ached, though I felt like pulling her arm off and beating her brains out with it. She pointed at the box on the back seat. I pulled it up front and lifted the lid.

"Pierrot! Very appropriate."

She pulled an envelope from her bag and gave it to me. "Your invitation. Are you scared, Paul? Excited — or what?"

I looked at her woodenly. "I'm as calm as a Wasaga trout in February. I guess you wouldn't know it, Uschi, but that's plenty calm."

Her cold blue eyes looked at me without expression. "I'm very glad. You'll need to be."

I gave her the same false smile. "And that's just for openers. Wait till I get warmed up."

"What are you going to do about Sophie?" she asked casually.

There was something about hearing the child's name in her mouth that bugged me. "I don't understand you," I said spikily.

She lit a cigarette from mine, considering the smear of lipstick on the end. "Well, it might be some time before the police allow us to go home. I was thinking that she'd be alone, that's all."

I shook my head decisively. "She won't be alone. The maid's going to sleep there tonight. What about you, Uschi? Don't you feel nervous at all?"

Sunshine slanted through the rear window, touching her face. She gave me a closed smile that could have been gentle but wasn't.

"No. I'm not nervous. You'll see, Paul."

She should have been an actress. All she needed was to round out her performances and she'd be a natural for an Oscar. I did a little acting of my own, leaking doubt into my voice.

"I've been wondering whether it's really going to work out. I mean us."

She smiled at me with everything but her eyes. "That de-

200

pends on how much we really want it. We've as much chance as anyone else."

I let my head droop a little, thinking indeed but anything but the thoughts she imagined. I looked up and squared my shoulders.

"There's nothing else, then, is there? We'll be at the house at nine-thirty sharp, radio time. You'll have left the kitchen door open and that about covers everything." I slipped the door catch back.

Her eyes flickered for the fraction of a second. The movement would have gone unnoticed if I hadn't been looking for it.

"Tell them to go straight into the kitchen. There won't be anyone on the grounds. I'm thinking about the man in Marika's suite. He just could be looking out of the window. They'll be carrying the gas with them?"

I moved my head in assent. "Then there's nothing else," she said, and offered her lips to be kissed. When I looked back from the corner the BMW had already gone.

The Scheinert School was a two-story building fronting a playground the size of a football field. There was a romp room and a cafeteria, and every kind of slide and swing outside. One of the girls in the office located Sophie on a goat sled. My daughter was trying to scare her steed out of its determined saunter. I took her into the cafeteria, where she settled for the usual scrambled egg and yogurt. I ordered a bowl of chile con carne. We were sitting at a window table, looking down at the other children. I knew more or less what I wanted to say to her, but the choice of words was difficult. I cleared my throat.

"We're off tonight, sweetheart, in Captain Baxter's airplane."

At Sophie's age one has the pragmatic approach to life. She licked the back of her fork, watching a small girl in a red beret beneath us. Sophie's tone was withering. "She's called Inge and she's a baby. She still pees her pants."

"Didn't you hear what I said?" I demanded. "We're going back to England."

She put her fork down, her interest awakened. "Back to Thames Court?"

"Just for a little while. How far back can you remember — things that happened a long time ago?"

She finished her milk, frowning. "Do you mean Spain, Papa?"

That had only been eight months before. I still had the pawn tickets that had transformed a Leica camera and a pair of Zeiss binoculars into two weeks at the noisiest dump in Tossa del Mar. I'd suffered, but Sophie had adored every moment of it.

"Before that," I urged.

She wiped her nose on the back of her hand, solemn eyed, and shook her head. What I had really wanted to know was if she remembered her mother. I'd always tried to deal fairly with the memory and Sophie had never revealed a sense of loss, nor had she ever probed beyond what I told her. But with kids you never know.

"It doesn't matter," I said. "First of all we'll be in Chelsea for a little while then we're going to the country, the way we always said we would. You'll like that won't you, sweetie pie?"

Her eyes were still serious. "It's O.K. if Eddie comes and stays. Then he can ride my pony."

I was getting into deep water but floundered on. "No matter what happens you'll remember that Papa loves you, won't you?"

She slipped down from her chair, gave me a cool peck, and put her nose against the windowpane.

"Can I go outside again now, Papa?"

It was as far as I could go. I picked up the box with the Pierrot costume.

"Sure. Don't talk to anyone about going to England tonight, understand?"

"I won't," she promised, pulling her hat down over her ears. Sophie is as close with a secret as a father confessor. My mind was easy on that score. The girl in the office assured me that Sophie would be back at the house before dark.

A leather-goods store downtown stayed open during the lunch hour. The sales clerk guaranteed that the Samsonite case would carry a hundredweight without collapsing. I packed the fancy-dress costume in it and carried the case a block north to the garage. I told a receptionist that the Rolls was being collected for shipment to England and gave him the car documents. A mechanic showed me a Mercedes 250 for hire. The trunk was big enough to take two men. I left a deposit and drove the car up the ramp to the gas pumps. I waited at the window while the attendant filled the tank. Twenty-five after one.

Chalice and Crying Eddie turned the corner. I drove down to meet them and they climbed in the back. I moved the hired car into the cobbled courtyard. The inn was busy with the lunchtime trade. I killed the motor.

"How about Pfeiffer?"

Chalice answered through a mouthful of apple. "He's up there now. We just seen him at the window."

Chalice fiddled with the recorder on his knee. Suddenly the speaker emitted a loud cough. It was so clear we might have been standing behind Pfeiffer in the bathroom. We heard a tap running, a toilet flush. Chalice switched off. He was his old self out of the black coat and striped trousers, relaxed and sure.

"So far so good, but it's a long time till tonight. We'll have to get that mike out of there before then — just in case."

I opened the car door. "It's a quarter to two. She'll be on time. She always is."

I stationed myself behind a delivery truck parked in front of the inn. The *Trinkhalle* was doing a brisk business, people coming and going. Another five minutes and the BMW nosed around the corner. Uschi parked outside the apartment. I watched her go inside and ran back to the Mercedes.

"O.K., we're on!"

We crowded on the front seat, Chalice turning a dial.

The first voice was Uschi's, speaking in German: "Did you get a good look at him?"

Muffled thuds that sounded like footsteps over the carpet. Creaks from the armchairs.

Pfeiffer, easily: "Good enough. He stood on the post-office steps for five minutes or more. But I didn't see anyone with him. You were the only person he talked to. He's tricky, Uschi. The moment he left your car, I lost him in the crowd."

A pause. Uschi again: "It doesn't matter. The other two will be coming through the kitchen with the gas. I think you're right about Henderson. He wasn't acting normally."

Pfeiffer, laughing: "He's probably nervous."

Uschi: "It was nothing I can put my finger on — a feeling more than anything. Did you manage to get everything done up there?"

204

Pfeiffer, grunting: "It was hard work. The ice is two feet thick. It took me the best part of an hour to saw out a good-size hole. It'll freeze by tonight, of course, but the crust will only be thin — easy to break."

A long silence, then Uschi: "You're sure no one saw you? I drove up there this morning. It's easy to see the lake if you look down from the bend and through the trees."

Pfeiffer, reassuringly: "Nobody uses the road after dark. There's nothing at the end but the ski lift. Don't fuss. If there's one thing I'm not going to do, it's stand trial for murder."

My whole body stiffened. Chalice looked up quickly. "What is it, mate? What are they saying?" I shook his hand off impatiently.

Uschi, doubtfully: "They're both big men."

Pfeiffer: "I wouldn't care if they were the size of elephants. A P-38 soon cuts them down to size. I've got a sled in the trunk of the car. It's only a hundred meters from the road to the lake. I'll get rid of the sled tracks on the way back. Don't worry, the bodies won't be found for three months — if then."

Uschi again, quietly: "No blood. There musn't be any bloodstains left in the kitchen."

More chair creaks. Pfeiffer, bored: "We've been through all this before, *Schatz*. The bags are waterproof."

Uschi: "Then I can think of nothing else that could go wrong."

Pfeiffer: "There *is* nothing, unless it's Henderson. I still think we ought to dispose of him at the same time. Three would be no more difficult than two."

Uschi, edgily: "That's complete lunacy, Helmut. I want him there when I denounce him to the police. A live suspect is better than a dead one — especially a live suspect like Henderson. A man known to the police, whose accomplices have escaped with the proceeds of the robbery."

Pfeiffer: "Yes. Yes, perhaps you're right. Let's get back to our timetable. I'll be in Basel by midnight, Paris by noon tomorrow. Don't phone Waldi's apartment under any circumstances."

Uschi, curtly: "I'm not that stupid. You're certain your brother won't be there?"

Pfeiffer, yawning: "He's in Hamburg till the end of next week. The concierge knows me and anyway I have a key. How soon do you think you'll be able to make it?"

Uschi: "With any luck Marika will fire me right away. But whatever happens, I'll be with you in two days at the outside. And don't worry about anyone following me. I know exactly what to do. By the way, those men will have the gas mask with them. I don't know which but one of them. It's better to take it first, isn't it? I mean a bullet might make it unusable."

Chair creaks. Pfeiffer: "Everything will be taken care of. I've got to collect the car. It's being serviced."

Uschi: "And I must get back to the Snow Queen. We won't see one another till Paris, Helmut. Be strong."

Sound of a kiss. Pfeiffer, confidently: "You too. You'd better go down now. I'll follow you out in a minute."

I reached the yard entrance just in time to see Uschi drive off. A moment afterward Pfeiffer emerged. He walked up the alleyway at the side of the post office.

I went back to the Mercedes and climbed into the driver's seat. I gave them the translation, word for word as I remembered it. A flush crept over Crying Eddie's face. Chalice simply sat there, cracking his knuckles till I had done. His voice was quietly incredulous.

"Did you hear that, Ed? This geezer's only getting ready to do us, mate. A hole in the head to start with and then the deep freeze!"

"A right pair of bastards," Eddie said grimly. "He's going to enjoy himself, stand on me."

"He's gone to collect his car," I said. "I'm going in for the mike. You two put the block on. Fall down in front of him if you have to, but don't let him into that apartment."

They went off in opposite directions as I crossed the street toward the photography store. The upstairs room smelled even stronger of Uschi's scent. I retrieved the mike from under the bottom drawer, opened the desk, and removed the picture of Pfeiffer and Uschi from his wallet. We all reached the car together.

"Let's go back to the house and talk," I said.

We passed the Porsche on its way down the hill, but Skomielna's mind was on other matters. He let the black Mercedes go by without giving it a second glance. The maid was in the small house, cleaning. I locked the front door and put the Samsonite case on the sofa. The fire had been lit. We sat down, facing one another.

"A council of war," said Chalice, pulling out one of his cheroots.

I nodded. "You want to know what I think?"

He flicked ash at the carpet, smearing it in with his shoe. "Yes," he said reasonably. "I want to hear what everyone thinks. It ain't that other slags haven't tried to kill me before. It's just that I never heard nobody talking about it. It's a funny kind of feeling and I don't like it."

I've been in my share of brawls. A drunk in a Yonge Street dive once offered to part my hair with a bottle. Somebody else finished an argument on the hockey rink by breaking my nose with a stick. But I'd never been exposed to the threat of death by violence. It was odd to find that while I didn't like the idea, I was less disturbed than I'd have thought possible. I watched my fingers as they flicked the lighter. They were perfectly steady.

"O.K. We all know what a hell of a lot of things have broken loose in this deal — things that none of us could have expected. But one thing in my mind is certain. And we ought to use it as a springboard. This pair mean exactly what they say. They're not bluffing an inch. They mean to kill you two off and bury me for the robbery. I'm not too sure how Uschi figures she'll swing it, but I am sure that she'll do it, given the chance."

Crying Eddie's face was stony with doubt. "What happened to all that stuff you were talking about yesterday — that there'd be no evidence against any of us and so forth?"

I shook my head. "I don't know. I'm betting that she still has a couple of surprises left, that's all."

"And so do we, mate." Chalice lifted himself up, looking at us meaningly. "What's the weakest point in their plan — when do they leave themselves wide open? Come on, now, either of you!"

I answered promptly. "Right at the beginning. The first minute after you open the kitchen door. Everything hangs on that; Pfeiffer will be waiting there for you. But he doesn't know that *you* know he'll be waiting!"

Chalice was moodily plucking at the crease in his pants leg. "Nobody never tried to do something like this to me and got away with it. That's what I keep thinking, over and over."

Crying Eddie said nothing, but his expression was enough. I didn't much care for the turn the conversation was taking.

"Well how do you think I feel?" I asked quietly.

"Tell us," said Eddie.

I showed them the picture of Uschi and Pfeiffer. "Hostile, that's how I feel. I'm leaving this where the law will find it."

Chalice puzzled for a moment. "How do you mean, *find* it?"

I told him, hoping that the idea would find approval. I knew only too well that either man was capable of killing Pfeiffer.

"What do you think, Ed?" asked Chalice. "Don't just sit there looking at the ceiling like a parson. Let's have the benefit of that brilliant brain, mate."

"Me think?" said Crying grimly. "I give that up a long time ago. And if I was you I'd stop talking about other people's brains and use your own."

"I know what I'd do with the bastards if I had my way," Chalice answered darkly. "Her as well as him. But we got no choice as things are. We'll do it your way, Paul."

Crying Eddie climbed to his feet. "Well, if that's all settled I'll go upstairs and get some kip."

The way he said it you'd have thought he was going to rest before going to the theater or something. But Chalice seemed to find it normal enough.

He and I carried out the gas to the car. He took the measurements of the trunk, making sure there was plenty of room there for him to half lie, half sit. He was much quieter, almost sullen, but like Crying completely relaxed. It came as no surprise when he said he thought he'd go upstairs and join his partner.

"You mean you guys are actually going to go up there and sleep?" I demanded, up tight like a piano wire myself.

He grinned, giving me an explanation that had a sort of delicacy about it — as though excusing himself for having a failing unknown to others. "Just a little shut-eye, mate, that's all. It helps me indigestion."

I sat down at Skomielna's desk and called the airfield for the last time. Baxter told me that the plane was already on the runway, gassed up and serviced.

"Twenty-two fifteen?" he replied. "Surely, Mr. Henderson. Everything will be ready. I'll have to be at the controls so I won't be able to come out and meet you. One of the girls at Swissair has promised to take care of your party. A Fräulein Huber — she'll be expecting you."

We were alone in the house now. The maid had been gone some time. The sun had dropped behind the mountains, leaving the blackbirds foraging for their last cropful before heading for their roosting places. The photograph albums on the shelves beside the desk were pictorial evidence of Skomielna's past. There must have been a dozen of them covering twice as many years and more. The first album went back to nineteen hundred and twenty. A picture showed a haughty-looking young man dressed in white flannels and a straw boater. He was leaning on the end of a punting pole. Another displayed him in a waisted cavalry uniform and sitting astride an Arab stallion. It was amazing to see how many beautiful women had passed through his life. Other photographs portrayed him jumping on horseback with them, waltzing them through Viennese nights, lolling in their arms aboard old-fashioned steam yachts. It was only the last four albums that showed the Prince solely in male company. I put the books back on the shelves, wondering what made a guy turn queer at the age of forty. There were many reasons, yet none in itself seemed viable.

It was four o'clock when the school bus delivered Sophie. She made her usual barging entrance, flushed and bright eyed, clutching a sticky mess in her hand. She wanted to know where everyone was and what they were doing. Sleeping, I said, and helped her off with her coat and hat. She rambled on about her day as I warmed a pan of milk. As always, I was relieved to see her back. There was no doting grandparent to come running to the rescue once I went. No staunch friend to grab Sophie's hand and take my place. There was nothing but the deed of trust sitting in Gordy Campbell's office. Whatever it is they say about stolen money being tainted, there's something about a numbered account that soon sterilizes it.

We sat in front of the fire for a while and I read to her. It must have been nearly six when I heard the Porsche stuttering up the driveway. I just managed to get the lights off in time. I was in no frame of mind to listen to the Prince's banter. I pulled Sophie over by the door and covered my lips with a warning finger. She nodded, standing perfectly still as the door handle slowly turned. Skomielna's voice came soft and insinuating.

"Paul? Are you there, Paul?"

Neither of us moved. After a few minutes, footsteps crunched back to the guesthouse. I peeped cautiously through the window. He was out again almost immediately, carrying a lace-and-velvet costume over his arm. He cranked himself into the Porsche and sat there, looking across at us, the Cossack hat tilted over his eyes. He seemed to make up his mind in a hurry and drove off in a shower of snow and gravel.

Sophie waltzed away delightedly, holding up the hem of her skirt. I sat in her room with her as she started getting her few things together. Time dragged on, the minutes hours and the hours an eternity. It was eight-thirty when the others came downstairs, gloved and wearing suede shoes with foam-rubber soles. Both men looked grim but refreshed. Chalice cracked a smile for Sophie, jiggling his fingers in an idiotic sort of way. She smiled back at him fondly. I took her chin, making her look up at me.

"Now you listen to me, sweetie pie. We've got to go out but we won't be long. Try to get some rest. Later on we're all taking off in Captain Baxter's airplane."

"Where for?" she asked.

"I'll leave the lights on," I continued, "and lock all the doors. If you don't want to sleep, watch television. You won't be scared, will you?"

She wrinkled her nose. "Of course I won't, silly. Are we going to England, Papa?"

I settled her in bed in her socks and underclothes, and switched on the television.

"Yes. Now remember what I told you and don't go wandering around the house. Hear now!"

I closed the door quietly. Eddie's hoarse whisper followed me accusingly in the darkness. "I thought you was going to get the maid to stay. It don't seem right to leave her like this."

We were halfway up the stone steps by now and Chalice

came to my rescue. "Why don't you try to use your head, mate. What would the maid be thinking by the end of the night?"

I went up to the bedroom and took one long last look. I had money and passport, the gas mask fastened to my belt. Chalice and Crying were outside waiting in the car. We sychronized our watches. Chalice was wearing a dark blue cashmere topcoat over his street clothes. Crying Eddie had covered his suit with the chauffeur's coat and he wore the cap. Underneath the clown's costume were my leather jacket and brown pants. We shook hands all around very solemnly.

"Good luck, mates," said Chalice. Crying Eddie started the motor.

The mountains ringing the valley were like mounds of salt under a star-dotted sky. Lines of cars were parked outside the eating places, bands were tuning up in the cellar *boîtes*, droshky bells sounded, muffled figures hurried through the freezing night. We were running ahead of schedule. Eddie pulled into the parking space behind the public library and cut his head lamps. A snowman with coals for eyes stood sentinel over the empty lot. Chalice and I lit up smokes. The road corkscrewed up through the pine forests to the plateau five hundred feet above our heads. We could see the blaze of light from where we sat. The only traffic would be bound for Shahpur. It was ten minutes short of nine when the first car passed us, a chauffeur-driven limousine carrying three women with hair like bird's nests. They were sitting bolt upright, as though riding broomsticks. A steady stream of vehicles followed. There was a constant whine of changing gears and snow tires above us. Suddenly a red Triumph streaked into view, going fast. Pfeiffer was behind the wheel.

He was wearing glare glasses, but I'd have known him in any disguise. He was obviously in a hurry.

"Let's go," I said quickly.

The parking lot was still deserted. Nobody in the passing cars noticed Chalice climb into the trunk of the Mercedes. I lowered the lid on him. Crying pulled off the lot and onto the road. We worked our way up the winding ascent. We'd negotiated maybe half a dozen bends when our head lamps picked up a flash of chrome among the trees.

I touched Eddie's shoulder. "Hold it!" He pulled the Mercedes to a careful halt. The Triumph had been left with its rear wheels resting on a pile of granite chips. I tried the doors. They were locked. I ran back to the Mercedes. A sudden flare of light illuminated the snow-fat trees on the bend below. Eddie had the Mercedes moving before the next car was on us. Another quarter-mile brought us to the lodge. The gates were open, a uniformed cop standing in the middle of the driveway. He held his hand up, signaling us to stop. He glanced inside the car, checked my invitation card, and then signaled us to proceed. I watched him in the driving mirror as we drove away. He didn't give us a second glance. Chinese lanterns were strung between the trees surrounding the concourse. We waited for a Cadillac with Venezuelan registration to deliver a party of cloaked and masked highwaymen. Security here was tighter. Two Slade agents opened and shut the door like a trap, inspecting each invitation card scrupulously. The taillights of the Cadillac vanished toward the polo field. One of the men on the door motioned Eddie forward.

"First right," I said. "And around the back to the garage." I opened the door and walked up the steps.

Fingers plucked my invitation card from my hand. The cop's eyes lifted to my face.

"Thank you, sir. You'll find the men's room over on the right. The ballroom doors will be closed at nine-thirty sharp."

The entrance hall was crowded. Maids were walking about carrying trays laden with champagne glasses. I'd left my topcoat in the car and pushed my way through the press of bodies looking for Uschi. There was no sign of her in the foyer. I shoved as far as the ballroom. The scene was like a stage set in some lavish production of *Arabian Nights*. Lines of mirrors repeated waves of soft colors as the light filters revolved. Flowers were everywhere. Roses, orchids, and gardenias sprouted from vases, decorated twenty or more windowsills. The gilt-bronze Indian statues were garlanded with yellow and red carnations. A platform had been erected at the far end of the ballroom. Painted wooden bars turned it into a gilded cage housing the paraphernalia of the discotheque. A dark-skinned girl inside the cage wore little more than a fringe and Turkish pants. She was gyrating her bare breasts and stomach muscles to unheard music.

Skomielna's Cavalier hat topped a group of people standing near the dais. Marika Bergen was there, a lavender-and-gray shepherdess with a crook glittering with jewels. She was talking to Arlette Shashoua, a slave girl wearing a diamond stomacher that had been made for one of Farouk's mistresses. Heads turned, automatically presenting their best profiles as the flashbulbs started popping. The photographers moved like high handicap trap shots, triggering their cameras as their targets greeted one another in a polyglot babble. The ballroom was gradually filling.

I drifted back to the hall and chose my time to step backward through the first green baize door. Once past the second door, the corridor was strangely silent. Lights shone in the detectives' sitting room but the light in the kitchen had been extinguished. My foam-rubber soles made no sound. I flattened myself against the wall outside the doorway. I could just see the illuminated hands of the clock over the kitchen dresser: nine-twenty.

I heard the yard door open. Two shapes were silhouetted against the window. The lights came on abruptly, catching Chalice and Crying halfway across the room. Chalice was carrying the gas cylinders; Crying had the Samsonite case. They put their loads down and lifted their arms in the air. I heard Pfeiffer's voice, curt and in English:

"Over by the wall!"

I could see no more than half his body, the back of his head, and the hand holding the P-38. The silencer made the barrel unnaturally long.

I reached around behind him and thumbed up the light switch. A violent struggle erupted in the darkness. I heard the gun skate across the floor, a cry of pain, a sickening thud as someone's head hit the ground. I snapped the lights on again. Pfeiffer was lying on his back, Eddie standing over him, massaging his knuckles. The German's eyes were open. Chalice bent down and smashed his fist deliberately into Pfeiffer's face. A worm of blood crawled from a nose that would never be the same again.

"Get his car keys," I said. Chalice threw them across to me. We used three rolls of surgical tape to bind Pfeiffer's wrists and ankles. Eddie wiped the German's nose with a dish rag and then gagged him with it. Anger had drained Crying's face of color, pinched his nose.

We ran for the furnace room, carrying the gas and the suitcase. A pair of wire cutters put both phone cables out of action. I pointed through the arch and opened up the inspection plates.

"Fire the cans in here — nine thirty-five on the dot — and close up again. As soon as the bodies stop falling I'll be out."

I pulled the baize door back an inch. There were no more than two or three couples left in the foyer. The cops were standing over by the front door. I was washing my hands in the men's room when I heard one of them calling.

"Everyone into the ballroom, please, ladies and gentlemen. Everyone inside, please!

"And I hope she falls on her lousy duff!" he added in a quieter voice.

The whole staff assembled with the guests, keeping to the end nearest the entrance. Skomielna skipped to the center of the dance floor, clapping his hands for silence.

"People!" he fluted. "*Pee-pul!*" There was a momentary hush. "Will you all step back a little, please. Marika has paid me the honor of asking me to open the ball with her!"

He ignored the ironical applause, doffed his plumed hat, and bowed low to Bergen. She curtsied and placed the tips of her fingers on his right arm. A diamond necklace had been wound around the shaft of the shepherd's crook she was carrying in her left hand. She was wearing rings on all her fingers and both thumbs, rubies and diamonds. Her wrists were loaded with matching emerald bracelets, each a couple of inches wide. The pendant around her neck terminated in a pear-shaped stone of staggering brilliance.

She signaled to the girl in the cage. The first swelling

chords of Strauss silenced the murmurs in the crowd. The ballroom seemed to lean forward as Skomielna swung his partner into the Viennese waltz. Someone started to beat time with his palms — others took it up. Suddenly the room was filled with flying figures. Venetian boatmen, cancan dancers, Columbines, and the party of highwaymen. Victorian sidewhiskers nuzzled into baby-doll hairdos. A fat man in rompers, carrying a rattle, spun by clutching a woman whose green hair was adorned with jeweled snakes. I could see Uschi now, in black velvet and patches, Lady de Winter in *The Three Musketeers*. She was talking to one of the ex-kings from Estoril. I put myself in a position where she had to see me. A brief smile was her only acknowledgment. According to her plan, Chalice and Crying should have been in plastic bags by now, bleeding to death. Nine thirty-four.

I leaned back against the dais, groping behind me under the brocade curtain. The space beneath was empty. I lowered myself gradually and crawled under the curtain, unnoticed in the confusion of flying bodies. It was hot in there and the heavy gas mask made it worse. The air I was taking in tasted and smelled of sulfur. The stage shook overhead as the girl continued to gyrate. Nine thirty-seven.

The gas was already circulating in the air ducts. I heard a woman call for help. I crawled out from under the dais. Most of the dancers had already collapsed. Some of them still clung together. Those near the doors had taken a double dose of gas: there was a duct over each door. Cops, maids, and guests lay in an untidy heap. One woman had lost her wig. A cop had managed to get his gun halfway out of its holster before falling. An elderly maid was displaying blue

nylon pants trimmed with lace. The last guy to go was staggering near the wall, arms outstretched as if playing blind-
man's buff. He dropped to his knees as I watched, instinct
prompting him to protect his head as he slid forward. Two
hundred bodies lay prostrate on the dance floor. Women's
skirts were hiked up around the wearers' waists, bodices had
burst. A set of dentures grinned from under a chair. The
faces of the fallen were contorted in pain and dismay. A
man dressed as a monk was smiling faintly, as if the whole
thing were a joke to be shared. The music played on, louder
now without the noise of the dancers.

Skomielna and Bergen appeared to have lost consciousness
at the same time. They were lying on their backs, side by
side, like a carved knight and lady on some Norman tomb.
The diamond-draped crook lay between them. A small gold
purse was attached to Bergen's forearm by a chain. Inside
the purse was the safe key, a small flat piece of metal with
words on each side of the shank. I stepped over the prostrate
bodies, heading for the exit. The sound of the music followed me out into the hallway and echoed through the house.
I unlocked the front door. Nine-fifty.

Chalice and Eddie emerged from the corridor, grotesque
looking in their gas masks. Both were carrying guns. Pfeiffer
dangled over Chalice's left shoulder like a sack of potatoes.
I took the suitcase from Crying Eddie, holding the safe key
up for them to see. It was impossible to talk with the masks
on. We all knew what we had to do. We dragged Pfeiffer
into the ballroom, unfastened him, and took off his gag. The
other two held him up between them so that his face was
jammed against an air duct. His head had already started to
roll as I turned and made for the staircase. I opened the

door leading to Bergen's suite. The lights were on in the rose-colored sitting room. The first thing I noticed was the small round safe set in the wall and the empty chair in front of it. A man with a grizzled crewcut lay face down in the Persian carpet. Beside him on the floor were his spectacles and a copy of *Sports Illustrated*. The fall had broken his spectacles. His head lolled as I turned him over. I found the second key to the safe in his pants and opened up. The three shelves were crammed with jewel boxes. I emptied their contents into the steel-lined suitcase, a thousand facets winking in the light. Then I checked Marika's bedroom, but there was nothing worth taking in the drawers and closets.

The other two had located Uschi lying on the floor by the wall. The nails on her right hand were broken, as if she'd made one last desperate attempt to claw herself upright. They'd put Pfeiffer by her side. He was glassy-eyed and a million miles away. I got rid of my Pierrot costume and we dressed him in it. I stuck the two safe keys in his hip pocket, the picture of Uschi and him in Bergen's gold purse.

I signaled the others to fan out. Chalice moved to the far end, by the dais. Crying stationed himself near the entrance. I took the middle third of the room. We went to work, stripping the recumbent figures of their jewelry. I removed Bergen's pendant, the bracelets on her wrists, the rings from her fingers. We were only considering white, green, and red stones: diamonds, emeralds, and rubies. The pearls and bits of gold, the semi-precious stones we left. After ten minutes of it, my shirt was plastered to my back. It was hot anyway and I was unable to breathe properly in the mask. Each respiration only half filled my lungs, producing an agonizing feeling of claustrophobia. That and the constant bending were making my head dizzy. Another quarter-hour and we were done. Jewels cascaded into the reinforced suitcase, on and on till our pockets were emptied. We made for the exit. The record had changed and a bossa nova was blazing out across the prostrate bodies.

I opened the burner in the furnace room, protecting my face from the heat. The empty gas containers were molten metal in seconds. I sent the skeleton keys and burglar's tools to join them. We left by the kitchen, tearing our masks off the moment we stepped outside. The air tasted like chilled champagne. We stood there gasping it in, like fish floundering on a riverbank. I threw the suitcase into the Mercedes and we piled in after it. Crying Eddie put on his chauffeur's cap and coat. Chalice was in back with me. We followed the driveway, circled the rear of the house, and joined the lane that led to the polo field. We could just see the lines of parked cars in front of the marquee. The front of the house was still ablaze with lights, the lanterns glittered in the snow-covered trees. The lodge was dark and deserted.

We stopped at Pfeiffer's car. I used his keys and stuffed the gas masks under the driver's seat. It wasn't quite the last touch but almost — one way or another they were going to have to do a hell of a lot of explaining between them. Chalice grinned with delight as I climbed back beside him. He kicked the suitcase at our feet.

"Millions!" he said. "'Like the bleedin' Crown Jewels! We just made history, that's what!"

I couldn't bring myself to answer. It seemed to me that the wrong word might break the spell. I could only repeat the same thing over and over as we dropped down toward the village: *It's got to be right!* No cops came spilling out into the road as we took a left in front of the railroad station. The village looked normal enough — the bars and hotels crowded, Bahnhofstrasse a solid line of parked cars. Ten-ten P.M.

We nudged up through the gates and left the Mercedes in the driveway. The drawing room fire had burned down to a shell that collapsed as I opened the front door. I was halfway down the stone stairs when foreboding hit me like a bucket of birdshot. I started to run, calling Sophie's name. I burst into her room to see an empty bed. Her clothes were still on the chair and the television set had been turned off. The back of the casing was cold. I called up the stairs, my voice cracking. The other two came flying down on the run. I pointed at the empty bed. The words seemed to hang in the air like balloons in a comic strip.

"Pfeiffer's got her!"

They were gone in a flash. I could hear them upstairs, running from room to room, opening closet doors, shouting to one another. My mouth was dry and bitter. I dragged up the stairs to the gallery and dropped into a chair. Chalice's voice came from a great distance.

"Come on, mate — pull yourself together and listen to me. A window's been broke in the kitchen — that's where he come through — and he let himself out the back way. He must have been waiting for us to leave, nipped straight in, and took her back to his place. That's why your bleedin' baroness was so sure you'd stay!"

Eddie's face came into focus. "That's the only place she can be. He wouldn't have no time for anything else. Don't forget he passed us on the way up."

I vaguely remember locking the door as we left, the long

sideways skid as Eddie trod hard on the accelerator. We hit the gatepost, crumpling a fender. As far as I was concerned it might have been a breaking twig. Chalice lit a cigarette and stuck it between my lips.

"Don't worry, mate. We're going to get her back."

The village lights were becoming brighter with each bend. I could only think of Sophie. Sophie, Sophie, Sophie — till I could stand it no more. I leaned forward and touched Eddie on the shoulder.

"Hold it here, Eddie. I want you both to listen to me."

"Do as he says," Chalice ordered.

Crying Eddie came down through the gears to a smooth stop. The clock on the dashboard already showed a quarter after ten.

"What is it, mate?" Chalice asked quietly.

I tried to make them understand. "We've done what we came to do. We're sitting on a fortune. You both know how much I need this score, but Sophie's my problem not yours. What I'm trying to say is that she might not be in Pfeiffer's apartment. I can't leave but I want you two to get on that plane and blow. I'm asking this as a friend. Then at least we won't have risked our liberty for nothing."

Crying Eddie bundled his cap in the livery topcoat and dropped them behind the front seat. He wiped his nose carefully.

"What's that supposed to be, some kind of a joke?"

Chalice's clenched fist thumped my knee. "Nobody's leaving anyone. Let's move, Ed!" Ten-twenty P.M.

The only sign of life along Seestrasse was at the inn. The windows of Pfeiffer's apartment were in darkness. Eddie drew up directly in front and stayed at the wheel, keeping the motor running. Chalice crossed the sidewalk with me. The skeleton key that fitted the door had gone with the rest of the equipment. I'd left Pfeiffer's house keys on the bunch in the Triumph.

"Rev the motor," I shouted to Crying. I braced myself against Chalice and kicked at the lock as the motor roared. Wood splintered. The second kick tore the lock free. I flew upstairs to find yet another empty room. It had been an act of faith that I would find Sophie there. Hope ebbed away. Suddenly my eyes found a patch of color in the light coming from the streetlamp outside. Sophie's rubber doll was propped up in the armchair. I grabbed it, everything clear to me. Chalice's face tightened as he saw me descending the stairs alone. I showed him the doll and sprinted across the street to the inn as Eddie started to turn the Mercedes. I made it across the courtyard, sliding and stumbling.

A thick haze of tobacco smoke hung beyond the leather curtain. I shouldered my way through the crowd standing around the zither player and into the room beyond. The three men there looked as if they hadn't changed position since I'd last seen them. All gave me the same blank stare.

"Where's the girl?" I said hoarsely.

The landlord moved his head with the indolence of a snail, not bothering to speak. I threw the door wide. It was difficult to see at first through the smoke and the steam. Great vats of liquid were bubbling on an open range. Blackened hams and strings of sausages hung from the ceiling near the fireplace. A tired-looking woman was sitting at a table littered with coloring crayons. I recognized her as the woman who cleaned Pfeiffer's apartment. Sophie and I saw one another at the same time. She wriggled down from the woman's lap and up into my arms. She clung tightly to me, whimpering.

The landlord's daughter rose, a troubled look on her face. "The gentleman is angry? But I had no idea . . . I took the laundry across to Herr Pfeiffer's apartment and the child was crying . . ."

I didn't wait to hear the end but lifted Sophie and ran for it. She was still dressed in her underclothes and without shoes. Crying Eddie had drawn the Mercedes across the yard entrance, blocking anyone who might have come after us. Chalice's strong arms took Sophie from me and the car shot forward. When I opened my eyes again we had stopped in front of the railroad station.

"The phone call," Chalice reminded.

My brain was beginning to work again. The booking hall and tracks were crowded with skiers taking the last train back to Zürich. I walked into one of the phone booths and called the Todtsee Fire Department. A man's voice answered promptly.

"There's a fire at Shahpur," I said. "Come quickly."

I heard a bell ringing loudly in the background as I hung up. It was our last card. In a few more minutes the police would be on their way up the mountain. None of the guests would make any sense for the next two hours. By that time the police would have come to their own conclusions about Uschi and Pfeiffer. Ten thirty-five.

The terminal building was lit. I could see nobody in the hall but a Swissair hostess and a couple of airport policemen. I took the car keys from Eddie.

"Let me do the talking."

There were no porters on duty. We carried in our own

bags. Sophie was wrapped in my topcoat. The case containing the jewels was tucked under Chalice's arm. Footsteps clicked across the deserted hall toward us. A hostess in a cloak greeted us brightly.

"Mr. Henderson?"

I gave her the car keys. "There's a car outside belonging to Engadine Hire. Give them a ring in the morning and they'll send a man to collect it. Have you got a rug or something for the child?"

She looked at Sophie with concern and nodded. "I'll get you something right away, sir. Will you take your bags and passports to the customs barrier, please? Your plane is waiting for you."

The two cops were fifty feet away, at a barrier near the exit. Chalice and Crying gave me their passports. We walked across the hall, meeting the hostess halfway. She gave me a blanket for Sophie.

"The passengers for the Beechcraft," she said in German.

The cop who held his hand out had a hatchet face devoid of humor. His voice was an angry bark.

"Passports!"

He flipped the pages slowly, looking at Sophie. "This is your daughter?" he asked in English.

I nodded. If I'd let go of the bag I was holding, I'd have shaken like a jellyfish.

He held out his hand again, palm upward. "Birth certificate."

"She's entered on my passport," I said. "Look — here!" I tried to show him where but his look discouraged me.

"You are all going to Paris, Herr Henderson?"

"That's right, all of us," I answered. A stupid question and a stupid answer. We were hardly likely to part company in midair.

He looked at Chalice and Crying, who were standing behind me wooden-faced. Then he let us through the barrier grudgingly. I have never seen anything more beautiful than the Beechcraft, black and silver in the moonlight. Baxter was standing at the top of the gangway, a huge grin on his face. A ground crew wrapped like Eskimos helped us up with the bags. I threw the blanket down to the hostess. The pressurized cabin was luxurious.

Baxter closed the hatch and held his raised thumb against the window. The chocks were removed from the wheels. The pilot turned around, still grinning. It was fairly obvious he was glad to be leaving Todstee.

"Welcome aboard! You'll find everything you need in the racks in front of you. Fasten your seatbelts, please, and keep them fastened till I give the O.K. And no smoking!"

He seated himself at the controls, leaving the door to the cockpit open. The plane shuddered under the impact of twin turbojets. Chalice had both feet on the case containing the jewelry. We taxied to the end of the runway. I braced Sophie in my arms, ready for takeoff. The motors stopped suddenly. A red button was blinking on the console in front of Baxter. A high-pitched *bleep* penetrated the cabin. The pilot twisted around, taking off his headphones. His voice was loud in the sudden silence.

"I'm sorry about that. They've told me to hang on. The customs officers are on their way out."

He didn't have to tell us. I could see the jeep tearing across the tarmac, head lamps full on. Chalice started to undo his topcoat, one button at a time, very slowly. Across the aisle, Crying Eddie was doing the same. The next move would be for their guns. It was too late now for me to try to stop them. Whatever happened I was part of it. Baxter strolled back, smiling reassuringly, and opened the hatch. A current of freezing air blew in. I heard the jeep stop, a door slam. Baxter looked back over his shoulder.

"It's you they want, Mr. Henderson."

Chalice's right eye flickered warningly. It was a thousand miles to the open hatch. I leaned out, looking down into the upturned face. The cop reached up, offering something with his hand. His ironical smile signaled the belated triumph of officialdom.

"Don't you usually take your passport with you?"

I took it in a daze and Baxter resealed the cabin. His freckled face was relieved. Chalice used his handkerchief surreptitiously on his forehead. Crying Eddie's eyes were shut tight.

"You had the wind behind you there, sir," Baxter observed. "Same thing happened to me in Bangkok last year. I got flustered at the checkpoint and forgot my passport. I landed in Rangoon without it and spent thirty-six hours in Immigration Control. I learned that there are forty-two ways of cooking rice in Burma and they serve warm beer with all of them."

He winked at Chalice, touching the top of Sophie's head as he went back into the cockpit. The motors whined and then roared to full throttle. The plane gathered speed and we lifted off into the air. I took the longest breath this side of the grave, as the undercarriage thudded up into place. The plane banked sharply, bucked like a mustang, and headed for a gap in the ring of bone-white mountains. The lights of Todtsee dwindled down to pin points and then vanished completely. We climbed steadily, passing into a realm of brilliant moonlight where there was no sound other than the steady grumble of the motors and an occasional crackle of static.

Chalice unfastened his seatbelt and wiped his forehead again, this time openly.

"After that I'm going to have another think about religion, mate. A real good long think."

Baxter's voice sounded in the speaker. "We're flying at a height of twenty thousand feet and our speed is two hundred eighty-five miles per hour. Our estimated time of arrival in Paris is twenty-three hours twenty, local time. The weather in Paris is cloudy and raining."

I touched the button over my head and Baxter looked around inquiringly.

"Find out what the weather's like in Brussels," I said.

"Brussels?" he repeated, puzzled.

"I changed my mind. That's where we're going."

His back was expressive but I could see him talking to someone beyond the cloud barriers.

Sophie stirred in my arms, her eyes half-open. "I liked it in Todtsee, Papa. Will we go back there one day?"

I glanced across at the others. Chalice had settled down with his book on Rommel. Crying Eddie's eyes were tightly closed.

"I doubt it, honey," I said. And I turned off the light. Seconds later she was sleeping peacefully, her hand clasped in mine.